Copyright © Willow Rose
Published by BUOY MEDIA

All rights reserved.

No part of this book may be reproduced, scanned, or distributed in any printed or electronic form without permission from the author.

This is a work of fiction. Any resemblance of characters to actual persons, living or dead is purely coincidental. The Author holds exclusive rights to this work. Unauthorized duplication is prohibited.

Cover design by Juan Villar Padron,
https://www.juanjpadron.com

Special thanks to my editor Janell Parque
http://janellparque.blogspot.com/

To be the first to hear about new releases and bargains from Willow Rose, sign up below to be on the VIP List. (I promise not to share your email with anyone else, and I won't clutter your inbox.)

- Tap here to sign up to be on the VIP LIST -

Tired of too many emails? Text the word: "willowrose" to 31996 to sign up to Willow's VIP text List to get a text alert with news about New Releases, Giveaways, Bargains and Free books from Willow.

Follow Willow Rose on BookBub:

Connect with Willow online:
Facebook
Twitter
GoodReads
willow-rose.net
madamewillowrose@gmail.com

facebook.com/willowredrose
twitter.com/madamwillowrose
instagram.com/madamewillowrose

Books by the Author

HARRY HUNTER MYSTERY SERIES

- All The Good Girls
- Run Girl Run
- No Other Way
- Never Walk Alone

MARY MILLS MYSTERY SERIES

- What Hurts the Most
- You Can Run
- You Can't Hide
- Careful Little Eyes

EVA RAE THOMAS MYSTERY SERIES

- So We Lie
- Don't Lie to me
- What you did
- Never Ever
- Say You Love me
- Let Me Go
- It's Not Over
- Not Dead yet
- To Die For
- Such A Good Girl
- Little Did She Know

EMMA FROST SERIES

- Itsy Bitsy Spider
- Miss Dolly had a Dolly
- Run, Run as Fast as You Can
- Cross Your Heart and Hope to Die
- Peek-a-Boo I See You
- Tweedledum and Tweedledee
- Easy as One, Two, Three
- There's No Place like Home
- Slenderman
- Where the Wild Roses Grow
- Waltzing Mathilda
- Drip Drop Dead
- Black Frost

JACK RYDER SERIES

- Hit the Road Jack
- Slip out the Back Jack
- The House that Jack Built
- Black Jack
- Girl Next Door
- Her Final Word
- Don't Tell

REBEKKA FRANCK SERIES

- One, Two…He is Coming for You
- Three, Four…Better Lock Your Door
- Five, Six…Grab your Crucifix
- Seven, Eight…Gonna Stay up Late
- Nine, Ten…Never Sleep Again

- Eleven, Twelve…Dig and Delve
- Thirteen, Fourteen…Little Boy Unseen
- Better Not Cry
- Ten Little Girls
- It Ends Here

MYSTERY/THRILLER/HORROR NOVELS

- Sorry Can't Save You
- In One Fell Swoop
- Umbrella Man
- Blackbird Fly
- To Hell in a Handbasket
- Edwina

HORROR SHORT-STORIES

- Mommy Dearest
- The Bird
- Better watch out
- Eenie, Meenie
- Rock-a-Bye Baby
- Nibble, Nibble, Crunch
- Humpty Dumpty
- Chain Letter

PARANORMAL SUSPENSE/ROMANCE NOVELS

- In Cold Blood
- The Surge
- Girl Divided

THE VAMPIRES OF SHADOW HILLS SERIES

- Flesh and Blood
- Blood and Fire
- Fire and Beauty
- Beauty and Beasts
- Beasts and Magic
- Magic and Witchcraft
- Witchcraft and War
- War and Order
- Order and Chaos
- Chaos and Courage

THE AFTERLIFE SERIES

- Beyond
- Serenity
- Endurance
- Courageous

THE WOLFBOY CHRONICLES

- A Gypsy Song
- I am WOLF

DAUGHTERS OF THE JAGUAR

- Savage
- Broken

LITTLE DID SHE KNOW

EVA RAE THOMAS MYSTERY - BOOK 10

WILLOW ROSE

We're all bad in someone's story.

- Unknown

Prologue
COCOA BEACH, FLORIDA

Health First Cape Canaveral Hospital 4 a.m.

LITTLE DID she know that this day would be the worst in her life. As she was rushed into the hospital hallways, moaning and grunting in pain while the baby made its way into this world, she was just so happy that the big, anticipated moment had finally arrived.

Sierra Holmes had gone seven days over her due date, and her stomach felt heavy and like a burden. She had barely been able to walk. She couldn't wait to meet her baby, the creature that had lived inside her for nine whole months.

She knew it would be worth both the wait and the pain.

"You're doing fine, sweetie. You got this."

Her mother's voice was encouraging and filled her with strength. Sierra had asked her to be with her in the delivery room since there was no dad involved. Now, she was holding her hand, looking down at her baby giving birth to a baby of her own. Her mother's eyes were soft and compassionate.

They hadn't exactly been like that when Sierra had told her she was pregnant. At only fifteen, it wasn't the news a mother wanted to hear from her daughter. And it had been quite surprising—shocking was probably a better word for it. Sierra wasn't the girl you'd typically expect to become one of the statistics of teen pregnancies. She was—and always had been—a straight-A student. She worked as a volunteer at the local animal shelter. She took only honors classes and became captain of the girls' soccer team just a few months before. She was one of the good girls. One of those that mothers talk proudly about when chatting with their friends. Sierra's mom would often brag loudly about her daughter.

Until the day her period didn't come.

Ever since she took the test and, while crying, showed it to her mother, things hadn't been the same. They had been fighting almost nonstop about it and how she could let this happen. They both agreed on only one thing: They were keeping the baby. No matter what.

Even though the father didn't want it, and his family left town without an address where to find them. They would take care of it together, her mother said. And Sierra would finish school no matter what. Her mother would see to that. This was just an obstacle, a bump in the road, but they could deal with it. Together, they would get through it, even though it was causing them to fight.

"Come on, sweetie; you can do it. One more push," her mom said, moving the hair from Sierra's sweaty forehead.

Sierra closed her eyes and pushed, letting her body completely take over, and she felt like she could have passed out at that moment when everything suddenly stopped. The pain was gone, and the overwhelming sensation of needing to push was too, and Sierra opened her eyes then looked at her mom. She was standing with the baby in her arms, crying.

"You did it, Sierra. You did it!"

"Eight pounds of sheer beauty," the nurse said, also smiling.

Sierra sighed, relieved when the baby started to cry, and then she cried too. Her mother placed the baby in her arms, and she looked down at the tiny lump of flesh.

Welcome to the world, little girl.

Then she cried even more.

"We're gonna be fine, just the two of us," she whispered gently to the very blue eyes staring up at her. Never had Sierra seen anything more beautiful, and never had she been happier.

She knew in this instant that her life had been changed forever. She would never be the same again. Nothing else mattered in the world except for this little child. This really was what life was all about, she thought, tears rolling down her cheeks.

"She's beautiful," her mother said and stood beside her bed, placing a warm hand on her shoulder. "Just like you were."

Sierra looked up at her mom with a soft smile, grateful that they weren't fighting anymore.

"Oh, Mom. I can't believe she's finally here. This is really my baby?"

"It sure is," her mom said, biting her lip. It was hard to understand that it was just a few hours ago when the two of them had fought incessantly over the fact that Sierra had been so stupid to get herself in this kind of trouble and how she would never trust her again. It was strange that it was the same trouble they were now both crying about in sheer happiness.

"Look at how close you both are already," her mom said, kissing Sierra's forehead gently.

"Nothing can separate you two now."

SIERRA STARED BLISSFULLY down at her baby in her arms. She couldn't take her eyes off her, and even though she was completely exhausted, it was like she couldn't get herself to close her eyes. She didn't want to miss even a single second of her daughter's life—not even a breath. It didn't matter how tired she was. They had taken her away for some tests of her heart, and those minutes had been awful for Sierra. It felt like torture to be separated—almost like she could die. So, when they finally brought her back and told her the doctor would need to look at the results before they'd know what they meant, she had cried and decided she wasn't going to let go of her again.

A nurse had come in later and told her she needed to sleep when the baby did, but Sierra simply couldn't do it. She wanted to hold the baby so tight and never let go.

"It's you and me forever," she whispered and kissed her forehead. "Nothing and no one else matters."

Sierra's mom had left her and gone home to get her two younger brothers up and ready for school. She would be back later in the afternoon, she had told her, once she got everything at home under control.

"Just make sure you rest."

Sierra's dad wasn't in the picture. He had left when Sierra was just five years old, and her twin brothers were still infants. Sierra hadn't seen him since he moved up north with some woman he had met. He had refused to pay child support, claiming Sierra's mother kept the children away from him, so her mom had to get by on her own salary, selling medical insurance while trying to fight him through the courts. But her father was a lawyer himself and knew how to drag it out until her mom gave up because she couldn't afford the lawyer bills piling up on top of having to provide for three children.

Sierra didn't need a father for her child. Not if that's what they did.

"You and I are fine on our own, aren't we…Desiree?"

Sierra smiled to herself. Yes, that was her name. Desiree. She hadn't been sure about it until this moment when the baby looked into her eyes and made a small squeak that sounded like crying but wasn't really. She truly was a Desiree.

The door opened, and a nurse peeked inside.

"Oh, good, you're still awake?"

Sierra didn't look up. She just stared at her baby and nodded. "Yeah. I can't stop looking at her, you know?"

The nurse approached her. "She's gorgeous."

"I know," Sierra said, tearing up again. She was so exhausted, yet she didn't want to sleep.

"I'm here to take her upstairs for some tests," the nurse said. "Then you can get some rest while she's gone. You need it."

Sierra felt uneasy at the thought. "More tests? Why?"

"Oh, don't worry. This is just standard testing. I'll have her right back in no time. But do try and get some rest while she's gone. You're gonna need it. Being a mom is no easy task."

The nurse reached down and took Desiree from Sierra's arms. It felt like her heart was being ripped out, and Sierra gasped lightly as the baby disappeared from her hands.

"Please…be careful with her…" she said, her voice trembling. "She's so…little."

The nurse smiled gently and held the baby close to her chest. "Don't worry. We do this all the time. Now, you rest, okay? Your young body has been through quite an ordeal. You'll need your strength to take care of this baby."

Sierra tried to calm her beating heart. She watched as the nurse carried the baby out of the room, then sat and stared at the door for a few minutes, her heart hammering in her chest. She was barely able to breathe.

The baby had been gone for less than five minutes. How could she miss her so deeply already? How could it hurt so much to be apart from her? How was it possible to love someone so much after only a few hours?

Try and get some sleep. You'll need it.

Sierra closed her eyes for just a few seconds, or at least that's how it felt. But when she opened them again, her mom was in the room, and as she looked at the clock, she saw that it was five in the afternoon.

"That was a good long nap," her mother said. "That's wonderful. You probably needed it."

Sierra sat up, trying to blink the fogginess away. She had been so deeply asleep; it took a while to remember where she was and what had happened. But then she did, and her eyes shot wide open.

"Desiree? Where is she?"

Her mom looked confused.

"What?"

"Desiree, my baby."

"You don't know where she is?" her mom said. "How can you not know where your baby is?"

"The nurse took her. For tests, she said."

Sierra was trying to fight the panic spreading like cancer through her body. It was like everything was about to explode inside her.

"Then that's probably where she is," her mom said, her voice calming down. "Let me go ask."

She went, then came back with another nurse. "They're asking which nurse took Desiree?"

"I…I don't know," Sierra stuttered while trying to remember. "She didn't say her name…."

"Well, what did she look like?" her mom asked.

Sierra felt confused. "She was in scrubs, she was…I don't know…tall, I think. I didn't really look at her. She just said Desiree needed to be taken upstairs for tests. That's all I remember."

The nurse shook her head. "Upstairs is the radiology department. I don't understand…why would she be taken up…" the nurse stopped herself, and Sierra saw fear rush over her face. "Let me just…let me go ask the others. Wait here."

"M-mom?" Sierra said as her mother approached her, putting a hand on her shoulder.

"Is Desiree okay?"

"I'm sure she's fine. I'm sure there is a logical explanation," she said.

But she struggled to keep her voice from trembling. No one else would notice that, but being her daughter, Sierra did.

And it scared her more than anything in the world.

Part I
CAMP HOLLY, MELBOURNE FLORIDA

Tuesday afternoon

Chapter 1

THE BUGS WERE BITING his neck, and Gary Johnson slapped one, feeling the sweat between his fingers. The sun burned down on him from above as he steered the airboat across the brown water. A black cloud—looking like the end of the world—was approaching, growing in the distance, telling him he needed to get the tourists back so they wouldn't get caught in the usual afternoon thunderstorm. The engine behind him roared as he sped up, feeling the sweat tickle as it ran down his back. In the bottom of the boat lay the dead four-foot gator he had just helped the tourist couple kill, then pull out of the water. It wasn't the biggest one, and he had hoped to go for another one, but the weather wasn't on his side. The thunderstorms were earlier than usual and building in size fast, too fast. Luckily, the tourists seemed proud and happy with their catch. Besides, they had gotten what they came for. They promised them a gator—one hundred percent guaranteed but never said anything about the size.

"We need to get back," he yelled, hoping they could hear him over the loud airboat engine. He pointed at the cloud in the distance.

"A storm is coming."

The couple nodded, the husband waving in agreement, and Gary steered the airboat through the trails in the water toward the camp and the docks. He glared up at the cloud growing in front of him like a massive tower of darkness, and now he could hear the rumbling thunder.

They still had about fifteen to twenty minutes before it hit them. It was time enough to get the couple back to the camp. It was Gary's first year as a guide, and so far, he hadn't been caught in a storm out on the water, but he knew others who had. His friend Pete had taken a family out a few weeks ago, and the engine had died in the middle of the swamps just as the storm hit. At first, the family had thought that he was just joking, trying to scare them. But as the realization sank in that they were stuck out on the swampy waters and a storm was approaching while they were sitting in a metal boat, they had panicked. Of course, Pete had called for help over the walkie-talkie and gotten ahold of the camp leader, who had come to them in another boat and taken all of them to safety. But the storm had hit first, and the lightning strikes had sizzled around them, causing the family to panic, and Pete as well.

From that day on, Pete stayed on land and worked at the gift shop, selling trinkets and drinks to the tourists instead.

"It's very close," the husband yelled at him. "Can we make it?"

Gary smiled the way his boss had taught him to, seeming as reassuring as possible and maybe even a little patronizing, making sure there was no doubt he had everything under control. After all, they did this all the time.

"Yes, we'll make it. Don't worry. We're fine."

But Gary wasn't as sure as he sounded. He felt the first raindrops hit his forehead, and the thunder was very close now. Lightning struck the ground not far away, and it sounded like the sky cracked. The wife whimpered anxiously, and Gary felt his heart hammering in his chest. He could see the camp now as he turned into a trail, then let the boat bump over a shallow area, then slide sideways before turning.

They were almost there.

And they were going to make it.

At least they would have if it hadn't been for the woman who suddenly screamed. Gary turned his head to look at her and saw that she was pointing at something. He looked at it and saw something in a dry patch area.

"Is that…" the woman screamed. "Is that a…girl?"

Chapter 2

"GO, ALEX, GO!"

I stared at my son as he ran with the ball. He had just started playing soccer recently, and it turned out he was really good at it.

My kid? Who would have thought?

Now, he was running solo down the field, losing the other kids completely. I was in awe. I had never seen him be into anything like this, maybe except his fire trucks and anything else with sirens and blinking lights.

"Yeah, Alex!"

And me? I had apparently become one of those super annoying parents standing on the sideline, yelling at my kid.

I didn't see that one coming either.

But, hey, when you're proud of your kid, then well…what can you do?

"Shooot, Alex! You've got this!"

Alex stopped, getting ready to take his shot at the goalie when another kid from the opposing team came storming toward him from the side, then tripped him just as he was about to make his move.

"HEY!"

I threw out my arms then turned to look at the people standing next to me. Alex fell to the ground, holding his leg in pain.

"Referee!"

I yelled as loud as I could while watching my kid on the ground, crying in pain.

"Nice job, T-dawg!"

The woman standing next to me was whistling and cheering on her son, the same boy who had just tripped mine. I stopped yelling then turned to look at her.

"That's your boy? He just tripped mine!"

She frowned. "No, he didn't. He just took the ball from him."

"My son is literally on the ground crying," I said.

"He's just acting. It's nothing."

I stared at her, my eyes growing wide. "It's nothing? Your kid deliberately hurts mine, and you say it's nothing?"

"It happens all the time. It's called playing soccer. Trent totally went for the ball. Your kid is just too wimpy." She whistled again loudly, then clapped. "Way to go, T-dawg!"

The boy turned his head and waved happily at his mom while I felt the anger rise in me. Alex's coach was attending to him now and looking at his leg; then, he helped him get up. Alex started limping toward me.

"Look at that. He's hurt. You happy now?" I asked the woman. "Your kid did that. Is that how you want to raise your kid? To be a bully?"

"Hey, if your kid can't take it, then he's got no business being on the field. He needs to toughen up."

I exhaled, annoyed. "Excuse me? You're not even going to address this with your son?"

The woman ignored me. I stared at the back of her, then tapped her shoulder, getting angrier and angrier.

"Excuse me?"

She still didn't turn around, so I tapped her again. Alex was limping closer, and the game continued behind him. Trent ran toward another kid and tripped him as soon as the referee looked the other way.

The kid went down, and Trent even stepped on his hand. The kid cried out in pain while Trent laughed and ran away, high-fiving a teammate.

"Did you see that? Is that the behavior you want to applaud in your kid?" I asked.

The woman still ignored me, and I felt so angry, so I tapped her on the shoulder once again.

That's when she finally turned around and placed a fist in my face.

Chapter 3

THEN:

They had been fighting for days, and Amelia was getting tired of saying the same things over and over again to her husband, Ron. Why couldn't he help her out more at night with the baby? Why couldn't he change a diaper just once in a while so she could rest?

"I'm exhausted," Ron said now and sat on the bed next to her, taking off his watch. "I'm constantly so tired."

"You're tired?" she said with a scoff. "You're not the one who has to get up three to four times at night."

He looked at her and sighed. "I would get up if I knew how to breastfeed and if I didn't have to go work in the morning. Someone has to make the money to keep you and the baby fed and living in this house."

Amelia rolled her eyes. That old song again. All she was asking for was just a bit more help with their newborn baby. It wasn't a lot to ask. It wasn't too much in her book. After all, her friend, Alice, who also just had her baby, had a husband who not only went to work and provided for the family but also got up at least once or twice at night so she could sleep.

"What?" he asked when seeing her rolling her eyes.

She looked down at her book that she wasn't even reading since she could barely focus on the letters.

"Never mind."

He exhaled and leaned back on his pillow, closing his eyes.

She put the book down with a scoff. "You're kidding me, right?"

He opened his eyes and looked at her. "What?"

"You're just going to go to sleep? You literally just got here. You didn't even call me to let me know you weren't going to be home for dinner."

He exhaled again, then rolled to the side, facing her while leaning his head on the palm of his hand. Then, he smiled that annoying endearing smile that she loved so much.

"I thought you were mad at me."

He let his fingers crawl under the covers and touched her thigh. Amelia smiled. She was so tired and wanted to say no, but as he looked up at her, his eyes begging, she couldn't.

She gave in, and they made love until they were stopped by the baby crying. Amelia put on her nightgown, then rushed in to check on baby Anna. She took her in her arms, then sat in the chair and breastfed her for about half an hour before the baby fell back into a deep sleep and she could put her down again. Amelia then snuck out of the room and down the stairs to get a glass of water. Ron had probably already passed out, so she checked that the front door was locked and turned out the lights in the kitchen before walking back up the stairs, wondering how many hours of sleep she would get tonight before baby Anna woke her up again with all her demands.

Then, she smiled to herself. Yes, she was exhausted by this, but having a baby was also the most wonderful thing in the entire world.

Amelia turned out the lights in the hallway and walked into the bedroom, where Ron was snoring lightly.

LITTLE DID SHE KNOW

She didn't even know she had forgotten to lock the back door, nor did she realize how fatal a mistake that was.

Chapter 4

IT BECAME PHYSICAL REAL FAST. I'm not proud to admit it, but after this woman slammed her fist into my nose, I pushed her. Not hard, but just enough to get her away from me. But then she came at me and pulled my ponytail hard. I screamed and tried to push her away again when the referee came running toward us, blowing his whistle aggressively, and we realized the game had stopped, and everyone was looking at us.

Including the kids.

I felt embarrassed. We weren't exactly setting the best example here. Alex was staring at me like I had just fallen from the moon.

I pulled back.

"What on earth are you two doing?" the referee asked. His face was red with exhaustion from running in the Florida heat.

"I'm...I'm...."

The way he looked at me made me even more embarrassed, and I stared at my feet, feeling like a child myself.

"I'm sorry," the other mom said. She was still panting. Her eyes were on me, and it felt like they could kill me.

"I'm sorry too," I said.

The referee looked down at us, then left. We watched him talk to the two coaches for a few minutes and then run back onto the field, setting the game back in motion. Alex sat down in the grass, pretending like he didn't know me. I couldn't blame him. I wouldn't want to know me either right now. Coach Finch came over toward me. The other team's coach walked toward the other mother.

Uh-oh. Now what?

"I'm sorry, Mrs. Thomas," Coach Finch said. "But they're really trying to strike hard on bad parent behavior these days."

"Bad parent behavior?"

I felt like I shrunk a few inches.

"Yes. It's happening too often. The clubs are required to give pretty harsh punishments for this type of behavior. They leave me with no choice, I'm afraid."

"What are you saying?" I asked.

Out of the corner of my eye, I could see the other mom arguing with her coach. She looked like she could punch him as well. My nose was still pounding from meeting with her fist, and I tried not to move it because it hurt.

"What do you mean by harsh punishments?"

Coach Finch sighed and ran a hand through his hair. He was a few years younger than me and quite good-looking. All the moms loved him. Plus, he was really good with the kids. I had always liked him, but I had never been in trouble before. I had never seen this look in his eyes before.

"I'm afraid I have to suspend Alex for the rest of the season."

My heart sank. Alex absolutely loved playing soccer.

"The…rest of the season?" I asked.

He threw out his arms and started to walk away. "I'm afraid there is nothing I can do. Those are the rules."

I stared after him, quite baffled. I turned to look at the other mother, who was now yelling at her coach, gesticulating widely.

I rushed toward Alex, grabbed his hand in mine, and walked back to the car just as my phone vibrated in my pocket.

Chapter 5

SHE CAME HOME and slammed the door shut behind her. Linda Smalls sighed deeply while her son ran upstairs to play. Linda sat down in the kitchen with a cup of coffee, then looked up at the calendar hanging on the fridge in front of her. She had marked this day by simply painting it black with a Sharpie like she did every year.

Linda felt tears in her eyes, then looked into her cup to try and avoid crying. She sipped some more coffee, then went to the fridge and pulled out the cake. She called for the boy to come back down.

"It's cake time."

"Yay," he said and ran down the stairs. He sat in the chair opposite her, and she served him a piece, tears rolling down her cheeks.

"Dig in."

"How old would my sister have been today?" he asked while chewing with his mouth open.

"Clarissa. Her name is Clarissa," she said with an exhale. "And she turns fourteen today."

Trent stared at his mom as she wiped away more tears and forced a smile.

"Now, eat."

"Can I have more when I'm done with this?" he asked.

Linda smiled. "Yes, of course, my love."

"But we can't eat all of it," he said.

"No, we can't."

"We have to leave some."

"Yes, sweetie."

She served him a second piece, and he inhaled it like she hadn't fed him in days. Then, he put the spoon down and smiled up at her.

"Can I go now?"

"We forgot to sing," Linda said.

"Oh, yeah," he said. "Silly us."

An uncomfortable silence spread in the kitchen before Linda finally managed to open her mouth and begin to sing.

"Happy birthday, dear Clarissa. Happy birthday to you."

The boy chimed in like he always did, even though he had never met his sister. He was used to celebrating her birthday every year. Sometimes, they'd go places, like to the zoo, or they'd even host a party in her honor. But that was mostly years ago when she was still young. Now, as the years passed, it was getting harder and harder for Linda to believe that Clarissa was still out there and that she would one day show up again. Still, Linda refused to give up hope.

That's also why, when the boy stormed out of the kitchen, she cut another piece of cake and put it on a plate, then lit the candle on top. She stared into the fire, then said, "Happy birthday, Clarissa," and blew it out while making her wish.

The same wish she had made every year since Clarissa was taken from her.

That her precious daughter would return home.

That this nightmare would end.

Linda smiled secretively when thinking of her baby before

walking to the fridge with the last piece of cake and placing it on a shelf as she did every year.

Saving it for her daughter, in case she came home.

Linda sighed and looked at the calendar, feeling sad. Another birthday had come and gone—another year without her daughter.

Fourteen years.

Would she even recognize her if she saw her in the street? Would she slam the door in her face if she came and knocked?

If only she had some clue that she was still alive.

If only.

Linda sat down heavily on her chair and finished her coffee, wondering what her daughter looked like now and if this nightmare would ever end when her phone lit up on the table in front of her, showing an unknown number. Thinking it was some spam call, she almost didn't pick up.

Yet something made her do it anyway.

Chapter 6

"SHERIFF DAWSON?"

I hurried through the hallways of First Health Hospital in Cape Canaveral. I spotted the Brevard County Sheriff at the entrance to a room. He was talking to someone. He saw me as I approached, then lit up.

"Eva Rae Thomas!"

We shook hands.

"So glad you could make it."

"I came as fast as I could get my mom to come over and babysit. What's going on? You said something about a girl?"

He exhaled and bobbed his head. "A couple of tourists who were gator-hunting in the swamps found her in a dry spot. She was just sitting there."

He walked me to the open door and let me peek inside. I saw a young girl lying in her bed, sleeping.

He handed me a file, and I looked into it. "It was almost a week ago?"

He nodded again. "It took us a few days to figure out who she was. We had to do DNA tests and everything."

"So, you know who she is?"

He nodded while looking secretive.

"Get this. Clarissa Smalls."

I lifted my gaze and met his eyes.

"As in Clarissa Smalls, the baby that disappeared from this very hospital fourteen years ago?"

"The very same."

"Oh, my," I said.

"We have notified the mother. I sent a patrol to pick her up."

I stared at him and his friendly blue eyes in the chubby face. "That's one for the books."

"It will be," he said, looking excited. "We're also having a press conference later, once mother and daughter have been reunited.

"So…why exactly do you need me?"

He grabbed my arm and pulled me aside as a couple walked past us, pushing their baby in a bassinet.

The sheriff spoke with a low voice. "Because there has been a situation—one we fear we can't solve on our own."

"And that is…?"

He sighed and rubbed his forehead. Sheriff Dawson was a good guy. He excelled at performing at fundraisers with his police dog and making people feel safe by making Facebook posts about criminals that his deputies had busted, especially if they had harmed animals. But he wasn't much of an investigator or even a policeman. He got stressed very easily and struggled to keep calm. I had worked with him on other cases before, and I knew him well.

"Another child has gone missing."

He spoke in almost a whisper now, leaning close to me, sweat springing from his forehead.

My eyes grew wide as I looked at him.

"Excuse me?"

"A newborn baby was taken two days ago from this hospital.

Only a few hours old. Just like Clarissa when she went missing fourteen years ago."

I could barely believe what I was hearing. My heart was racing in my chest. I could handle many things and had seen a lot in my line of work, but when it came to babies, I couldn't take it. Having a one-year-old at home didn't help.

"Another baby went missing? How? Why? What's wrong with the security in this hospital?"

He looked around nervously because I was being too loud. I lowered my voice and tried to calm down even though my heart was pounding in my chest with anger. How could something like this happen…twice? How could it happen at all?

"I'll fill you in on the details. But we need your help to find this baby, fast. And we're thinking that the solution lies with Clarissa, but so far, she has refused to say a word to us about where she has been. Maybe you can get her to say something, and then you could gather enough for a profile? The only problem is that we're kind of in a hurry. This baby that was taken was born with a very rare heart condition, and if she doesn't get surgery within the next few weeks, she won't survive."

Chapter 7

THEN:

She slept through the night. When Amelia woke up, it was already light out. She blinked her eyes, trying to get rid of the night and the dreams, then sat up. She couldn't hear any crying. Was the baby still sleeping?

That's a first.

Amelia looked at the baby monitor. It was dead. It had run out of batteries. She really should get a new one; this one kept dying on her. Then she looked at Ron's side of the bed. He was still sleeping, too, snoring lightly. Amelia exhaled, then looked at the clock next to her bed. It was eight. Anna had never slept this late. And she had most certainly never slept through the entire night without needing to be fed.

Amelia sat in the bed for a few seconds, wondering what to do. Anna wasn't crying now, so maybe it was a bad idea to go into the nursery? She would risk waking her. At the same time, she had a strange unease inside of her that was growing by the second. Could something be wrong?

The thought worried her, and after a little while, it became too much to bear. Once she got pregnant, Amelia had promised herself never to become like those mothers who worried constantly and would put a mirror under the baby's nose just to see if she was still breathing. Those women were nuts, she believed, and she swore she'd never end up like that. Yet, it had turned out to be a lot easier said than done. Because the worry was there, constantly, and so much could happen. They could fall asleep and never wake up.

The thought was absolutely terrifying.

Amelia got out of bed and walked into the hallway, her heart hammering in her chest as a thousand scenarios rushed through her mind.

Was Anna okay?

Relax, she just slept in. She's probably fine.

Amelia grabbed the door handle and took a deep breath, hoping she'd be able to open the door without waking the baby.

Please, let her be okay.

She opened the door carefully, trying to make as little noise as possible, then peeked inside. The bed was by the wall, but she couldn't see anything since the dark curtains were closed. Anna slept best in complete darkness. Amelia pushed the door open a little further, then tiptoed in. She reached the bed and looked inside of it. Then, her heart dropped.

It was empty.

The bed is empty! Why is it empty? Where's Anna?

Amelia could barely believe her own eyes, and turned on the nightlight next to the bed, then stared into the bed, blinking, before she put her searching hands inside like she expected the baby to be there somehow anyway. Frantically, she picked up Uncle Berry, the pink bear Anna had gotten as a present from Amelia's mother when she was born like she expected the baby to be hiding underneath him. Then she dropped him back into the bed as panic began to erupt.

"Anna?"

Maybe Ron took her? Maybe he moved her somewhere?

She turned around and rushed back to the bedroom. Ron was awake and looked at her.

"What's going on? You look so pale?"

"Do you have Anna?"

He wrinkled his forehead. "Anna? No, why…wait…."

He jumped out of bed. Amelia could feel how her entire body was shaking so terribly that she couldn't remain still.

"She's not in her bed, Ron. She's not in her bed. Where is she? WHERE?"

Chapter 8

"CLARISSA?"

I walked into the room. The young girl had woken up and stared at me as I entered. Her eyes were following my every move.

"Clarissa?" I said again.

She didn't react.

"She's been gone for fourteen years," Sheriff Dawson said. "We're not sure she even knows her name. Her kidnapper might have given her another."

I nodded. It made sense. She probably had a completely different identity.

"But she hasn't told you what she'd liked to be called?"

He shook his head. "Nope. She hasn't said a word since she got here."

"That's a tough one," I said.

"Yeah, we thought that well…since…you know…with your sister's story and all that, of her being kidnapped when you were kids and then coming back into your life thirty-something years later, that maybe you would know how to handle this."

I stared at him. I wasn't sure how that qualified me. I wasn't exactly a therapist.

"We already tried with several therapists," he said like had he read my mind. "They couldn't get through to her."

And you think I can?

"We're desperate," Dawson added with a deep sigh. "We've already lost several days, and the baby needs the surgery. The clock is ticking."

"What have the doctors said?" I asked. "How's her condition?"

"She's dehydrated but otherwise in great shape. They don't know how long she's been in the swamps, but they don't think she's been kept locked up inside or even suffered malnutrition. She's in good health."

"So, whoever took her took good care of her," I said. "For fourteen years."

He exhaled. "At least physically, yes. She's lightly bruised on her body, but that could be from surviving days in the swamps. But what else she may have suffered, we won't know about until she starts talking."

"Okay. I'll see what I can do," I said, taking a deep breath. A girl like her could have been raped or otherwise abused. It would explain her silence. She didn't trust anyone. "But I can't promise you anything."

"Of course not," he said smiling, relieved. He was putting a lot on my shoulders right now, and I had to admit it felt a little heavy.

Dawson left and took his deputies with him to give me privacy with the girl. They closed the door, and I grabbed a chair then sat down. Clarissa—I still called her that since it was the only name I knew for her—stared out the window. In the distance, you could see the cruise ships towering in the port. Alex, my eight-year-old son, was begging to go on a Disney cruise one day, but I wasn't sure I could afford it. Not the way things were right now, me being on my own with four children, one of them being a baby only almost a year old.

"I see you're looking at the cruise ships," I said and nodded at the windows. Clarissa didn't look at me. She continued to gaze out the window.

"My youngest is begging me to go on a Disney ship. Have you ever been on a cruise?"

She looked at me briefly, and I thought I had a breakthrough, but she then turned to the other side, turning her back to me again, making sure I realized this wasn't going to be easy.

"Okay, no small talk, I get it," I said. "But then maybe you could...."

I was midsentence when I heard voices coming from out in the hallway, and I paused. The door was pushed open a second later, and a woman stepped inside. I could have screamed the second our eyes met.

Chapter 9

"WHAT'S **SHE** DOING HERE?"

Linda stared at the red-haired woman in front of her. It felt surreal to see her there, but everything about this whole situation was completely bizarre, so she decided to ignore the woman and rush toward the bed, heart knocking against her ribcage.

Was it really true? Was it really her daughter? She didn't dare to believe it.

Linda hesitated as she came closer. Her body was trembling. For fourteen years, she had waited for this call. She had dreamed of seeing her again. Yet now that she was about to, she couldn't move.

"C-Clarissa?"

Linda clasped her mouth in order not to cry. The girl in the bed looked at her, her brown eyes barely reacting. Linda fought to keep the tears at bay as she stared at the young girl in the bed. She was so grown up, looking almost like an adult. She looked nothing like she had thought she would. Yet she immediately knew that it was her. As soon as their eyes met, she just knew.

A blissful smile spread across her face as she dared to move closer.

"Is it really…is it you…Clarissa?"

Sheriff Dawson was right behind her, and he cleared his throat. "As I told you before we walked in, she doesn't seem to…."

"Recognize her name; yes, you said that. But what do I call her then? And why doesn't she recognize me?"

Dawson tilted his head slightly, and it annoyed Linda. She felt so desperate, so vulnerable because this was nothing like she had imagined it to be. She had thought about this moment so many times, going over it again and again in her mind, and in her happy ending, Clarissa would cry and hug her, and they would never let go of each other again.

Never.

"As we told you, she hasn't spoken a word to any of us since she was found," the sheriff explained.

"And you must remember that she hasn't seen you since she was just a few hours old."

The last part came from the red-haired woman. Linda turned around and looked at her, eyes on fire.

"I didn't ask for your opinion. If I want to hear from you, I'll say so."

"Sorry," she said and pulled back, raising both her hands resignedly. "I was only trying to help."

Linda sighed deeply and rubbed her forehead. "I just thought that…you know…I'm her mother. I thought she would know when we…looked into each other's eyes. I just thought that…."

Linda closed her eyes briefly to stay calm. She felt like breaking into tears, but she couldn't let herself do that. Not here. Not with all these people around her, watching. She had dropped Trent off with a neighbor because she wanted to face this on her own and wanted to make absolutely sure it was actually her daughter before the boy was told what was going on. Now, she was happy that she hadn't brought him since this was an utter nightmare.

"Clarissa? Sweetie?" she said and walked up to the side of the bed. She took the girl's hand in hers and squeezed it tightly. Her torso was jerking because she was holding back the tears, but they wanted to come out.

"It's me. I'm your mom."

Clarissa looked into her eyes as the words fell, and Linda saw a reaction in them. Clarissa's lips parted, and a strong and powerful voice for such a little girl said, "You're *not* my mother."

Chapter 10

I COULDN'T BELIEVE the scene I was watching. This poor woman was holding her long-lost daughter's hand for the first time in fourteen years, and those were the words she spoke to her.

You're not my mother.

That had to hurt.

As the words fell, Linda Smalls let out a small gasp, let go of the girl's hand, and clasped her chest. My first reaction was to rush to her and grab her in my arms, but given our history, I knew I was the last one she wanted a hug from. So I stayed where I was.

Sheriff Dawson looked at me briefly, and I could tell he was surprised to hear the girl talk. It was the first thing she had said since she was rescued from the swamps; it just wasn't exactly what people wanted to hear.

"Yes, I am," Linda said, her voice high-pitched and desperate. "I *am* your mother. I gave birth to you in this very hospital, and you were taken from me."

The girl looked at her, then shook her head. "You're not my mother, and you never will be."

Linda smalls took a step back, and I could tell how she was

fighting her tears yet refusing to give in to them. Linda stared at her daughter, her body trembling.

"But…but Clarissa…"

"That's not my name! Stop calling me that!"

"Then tell us what your real name is," I said, stepping forward, keeping my voice calm so I wouldn't upset her further. Finally, we had the girl talking, so it was about getting information out of her as fast as possible. A baby's life was on the line.

The girl stared at me, then sank back into the bed, arms crossed over her chest. She turned her head to the side and ignored me. Her silent treatment puzzled me.

"Okay," I said. "You're not willing to help us out. I guess we'll call you Clarissa until you tell us what name you go by."

I saw her shoulders twist slightly, but she remained silent. I noticed that her hair had been cut recently, and it seemed like it had been professionally done. Nothing about her appearance made me believe she had been neglected, and I realized that might be why she didn't want to talk to us and tell us who took her.

She cared for her kidnapper. She looked at them as a caretaker and had a child's loyalty toward them like they were her parent.

Stockholm syndrome.

It wasn't unusual, especially when she had been gone for so long. It was all she had known.

Sheriff Dawson touched Linda's shoulder. "Let's go outside and talk a little. Your daughter needs rest."

Linda nodded with a small inhale. "I'll be back, Clarissa. I'll be back soon, okay?"

Clarissa didn't even look at her but kept staring out the window, ignoring all of us. I followed them out into the hallway, and Linda stared at me as I did.

"What do you think you're doing?" she asked me. "Why are you here?"

Sheriff Dawson looked at her. "This is FBI profiler Eva Rae Thomas; she's here to help on this case."

Linda shook her head. "Nope. She's not."

"Excuse me?" he said. "Do you two know one another?"

"You could say we might have bumped into each other," I said and touched my face where she had planted her fist earlier in the day. Luckily, it hadn't left much of a visible bruise. She hadn't hit me that hard.

Linda placed her hands at her sides. "You do realize that what you did got my son suspended for the rest of the soccer season?"

"The same happened to my son."

"Yeah, but for my son, soccer is his entire life. He's going for a scholarship, and he has the potential to become a pro. I'm homeschooling him for that same reason, so he can focus on his sports. It's his entire life and future, and now you ruined it completely."

I stared at her, not knowing how to respond. Should I tell her that I found it ridiculous to talk about an eight-year-old's career? Or should I tell her I was sorry since I needed her acceptance of my presence here in order to help save the baby? Clarissa—or whatever her name was—held the key to finding Desiree, the kidnapped baby.

Sheriff Dawson looked from one to the other, visibly confused.

"Eva Rae Thomas is our…"

"I don't want her anywhere near my daughter," Linda said and pointed at me. "I don't care how amazing she is. She needs to go."

Chapter 11

THEN:

Detectives Brent and Garcia approached the front porch with heavy steps, bracing themselves for what waited for them inside. Brent, who was the oldest and the one with the most experience with his more than twenty years as a detective, glanced at his younger colleague and then sighed.

"You ready for this?'

Garcia nodded.

"I'm only concerned because I know you have young ones at home yourself. Mine are grown and gone years ago, and I have been through cases like this before. I know how tough they can be on you."

Garcia looked up at his older colleague, then nodded. "I can take it."

"Good. Because I need you on your toes for this one—a missing baby is no walk in the park."

Garcia exhaled. "I don't expect it to be."

Brent cleared his throat, pulled up his pants, then walked to the door and greeted the officer standing in the doorway with a casual yet serious nod while showing him his badge. The street was blocked off, and an ocean of police cars was parked outside the house.

"Now, remember, the mother is one of us," Brent said with a low voice. "That makes it personal."

Garcia nodded. "She's a local cop; I got that. She is currently on leave to take care of her baby."

Brent walked into the kitchen, then nodded to a couple of officers standing there and spotted the couple sitting by the dining table, deep shock in their glassy, staring eyes. Brent and Garcia shook hands with the father, who got up and greeted them. The wife remained still, her fingers tapping on the table.

"Honey, the detectives are here."

She looked up at them, mouth gaping, almost like she didn't have the strength to close it.

"Thank God."

"Ma'am," Brent said. "We're gonna do everything we can to find your baby, Anna. It's our highest priority right now."

"Call me Amelia," she said, a glimmer of hope rising in her voice. "Do you have any news? Anything at all?"

He smiled compassionately, knowing this woman needed hope more than anything now. The baby had been missing for more than twelve hours, they believed, and every second counted. Brent thought about his own children when they were younger and knew it would have killed his wife to be in a similar situation. It was just worse than anything else when it had to do with little children.

"We've got a few leads," he said, trying to sound convincing. It wasn't a lie, but it wasn't the complete truth either. The fact was, there was no sign of an intruder entering the house anywhere. But the back door was unlocked, and if anyone had entered, it had to have been through there.

One of the horrible parts about these types of cases, crimes involving children, was that it was committed by someone close to them more often than not. Brent had seen several cases like this one, and he knew not to be blind to the obvious.

Brent turned to look at the father, then forced a smile.

"We will need to talk to each of you separately. Let's start with you, shall we?"

Chapter 12

SHERIFF DAWSON WAS PLEADING my case. I had to give him that. He was arguing loudly with Linda Smalls, and their voices echoed down the hallway while he explained to her how she was lucky to have someone with my expertise and experience dealing with her daughter.

"If anyone can find out who took your daughter, it's her," I heard him say as I slowly walked away. "She's the best in her field."

I heard him continue to explain to Linda Smalls how this was an emergency and how urgent it was to find this kidnapper, as another child had been taken, one that needed to have medical attention as soon as possible.

Meanwhile, I snuck down the hallway while they didn't notice me and walked into Clarissa's room. The girl looked at me with defiance.

"What I can't seem to figure out," I said. "Is whether you're trying to protect him because you think he's a parent or if you fell in love with him."

She didn't respond. I didn't expect her to.

"Either way, you love him, don't you? That's why you won't tell us who he is, or even where you've been, am I right?"

Her eyes grew softer, and she turned her head away.

"It's okay," I said. "I understand. It must be hard for you. You grew up with him, in his house probably."

I waited for a second to see if she reacted to the word house. She didn't.

"Or maybe in his basement?"

She turned her head and looked at me. I searched her eyes to find out if I had hit a nerve. Then she shook her head.

"You think you're so smart, don't you?"

I got her talking; that was a start, I thought to myself. Even though she had an attitude, it was better than the silence. I had teenagers at home, two of them, both girls. I knew the drill.

"As a matter of fact, I do," I said. "And I also think you're very intelligent. How did you become so smart? What school did you go to?"

"I was homeschooled," she said.

"Oh, really? I tried that with my oldest daughter once, but it ended terribly. We fought all the time, and I had to send her back. Do you know what I mean? Did you two fight?"

She looked down, then shook her head.

"Okay, so you could handle it. Maybe it was just harder for me because I'm the mother, you know? Girl to girl can be hard. I think it might be easier if her dad had taught her, don't you?"

Come on; tell me if you were kept with a man or a woman. You can give me that much, at least.

"Maybe it would have been better," she said with a light shrug.

"Yeah, because men are just easier to be around, right?"

She nodded and looked away.

Okay, so she has been around a man. That much is confirmed. And he homeschooled her. Not much to go by, but it's a start.

"Did you ever have to take the FSA? I know my kids have to

take it in the spring," I said. "You have to pass it even when home-schooled, right?"

She looked at me, and I could tell she had no idea what I was talking about.

"The Florida Standard Assessment?" I asked.

"I don't know what you're talking about," she said with an exhale. "Please, go. I'm tired."

"Just one more thing. That necklace you're wearing."

"What about it?"

She pulled it out so I could see it very close.

"Did you earn that?"

She nodded. "Just leave now, will you?"

Chapter 13

THE BABY WAS CRYING, and he went to take her up from her crib. He held her head gently and hugged her against his chest.

"There, there, little one. Everything will be just fine."

He tried to give her the bottle again, but she wouldn't take it. It worried him. She hadn't been eating a lot since she got to his house. She was such a small creature, and she needed nourishment.

"Let's try again, shall we?" he sang and put the bottle on her lips again, just the way he had done it fourteen years ago with baby Cate. He recalled that it had taken her a while to get used to the bottle too. But eventually, she had learned, and after that, she ate like there was no tomorrow.

He chuckled at the memory, and immediately his mind was flooded with images of Cate and the wonderful childhood she had spent with him. It was too bad it had to end.

But that was life, right? It had its seasons and sometimes those seasons ended before you realized they were over.

"That's not gonna happen with you, my little sweetheart, right?" he said to the baby, still trying to get her to take the bottle.

She spat it out again, and he shook his head.

"Why won't you eat?"

The baby cried, and he realized she had to be starving.

"It's right here, you silly goose. Just take it," he said and put the bottle against her lips once more. A drop of formula landed on her tongue, and he hoped that would make her change her mind.

"That's it, my love. Taste that wonderful dinner that daddy made for you."

The baby started to cry even louder, and he bounced her back and forth to calm her down, then placed the bottle against her lips again, feeling frustrated. He didn't remember Cate being this stubborn. Or maybe it was just so long ago that he had forgotten what it was like with her.

"Gotta have patience. I know. Patience is the key with you little ones."

He pressed the bottle against her lips again, and this time she let it slide through without pushing it back out with her tongue.

He felt himself ease up, and joy spread through his body, wiping out the worry that was growing in his stomach.

'That's it, my sweet girl. You drink that beautiful formula and grow big and strong for me."

The baby's eyes lingered on him as she finally figured out how to get the food out, and his heart melted as he looked deeply into them.

"You and I, we're gonna have so much fun together, aren't we? I have a feeling we're gonna be the best of friends."

He chuckled as the baby drank from the bottle, and relief filled him. Then she pushed the tip out from between her lips, and some formula ran down her chin. He wiped it off with a soft smile and then looked at the precious child he was holding in his arms.

"We're gonna need a name for you, aren't we? I was thinking Sandra. How does that sound to you, huh? Okay, then. Sandra, it is. Yes, it is."

Chapter 14

I SNUCK out of the hospital room without Linda Smalls seeing me and approached Sheriff Dawson. I pulled him to the side.

"She wasn't kept here in Florida by the kidnapper," I said. "I think she was in another state."

He gave me a look. "How'd you figure?"

"I got her talking a little, and she said she was homeschooled but didn't know the FSA, the Florida Standard Assessment that all kids take at the end of the year, even homeschooled ones. She seemed like she had never heard of it."

Dawson tipped his head. "Could just be that her kidnapper didn't want her in the school system. Plus, it would require a social security number, and he might not have had that."

I nodded. "Fair point, but there's more."

He looked at his feet briefly, then up at me. "And that is?"

"She's wearing a necklace."

He nodded. "I noticed that."

"I've seen that logo before. ICB stands for Inner-City Boxing."

"Really?"

"I used to live in Washington DC, and my best friend's son took boxing lessons there. He had a necklace just like it. You earn it after reaching a certain level or something. I don't know the details, but it's the exact same necklace."

Our eyes met. "You're telling me she's been in DC?"

"I'm saying it's a possibility. It's a start."

Dawson gave me a look, then grabbed his phone. He tapped on it then looked at me again.

"Seems that there are several ICB clubs located in three cities in three states. There's one in Washington DC, one in Boise, and one in Topeka."

"Okay, so it could be in one of those three areas. I know it's not much, but it's a start."

He nodded. "Okay. We'll look into it. Send her picture to the locations and have them talk to the local clubs to see if she went there."

"I don't have much on a profile of the guy yet, but I'm pretty sure it's a man. I also believe he has been taking very good care of her. She's educated and smart, and even her hair and nails are nicely done by a professional. My guess is he's not someone who wishes to harm the baby, which is good news. He also managed to make Clarissa either fall for him or look at him as a parent. And that's why she won't talk. She feels loyalty to the only grown-up she has ever known."

Dawson nodded. "That makes sense."

"But it also means it'll be very hard to find him since he knows how to avoid being seen. He managed to keep Clarissa somewhere for fourteen years, schooling her, taking her to sports, the hairdresser, and the nail salon without anyone asking questions. He made her think he loved her, which is probably why her loyalty to him is so strong. He hasn't harmed her. That wasn't his motive for kidnapping her."

Dawson exhaled as a doctor approached us and pulled him

aside. He came back a few seconds later, wiping sweat off his forehead with a napkin.

"Apparently, there is another aspect to this story," he said.

"And that is?"

He looked into my eyes, and I could tell he was devastated.

"She's pregnant."

"Pregnant?"

"Which means your little friend, *Mr. I-don't-want-to-harm-her* most likely raped her."

Part II

One day later

Chapter 15

COFFEE WAS my friend this morning. I hadn't slept much as I had gotten back really late. On top of that, Angel—my almost one-year-old baby—thought it would be fun to get up for two hours in the middle of the night and just start blabbering. It was adorable and made me laugh, but after two hours, it got tiresome. She was the cutest thing, and she knew it. She had taken a few steps on her own, and it wouldn't be long before she was running around all over the place, me chasing after her constantly. Luckily, her dad, my ex-boyfriend Matt had taken her this morning, and she'd stay with him for the next two days, giving me some time to work on the case and hopefully get some sleep as well. Linda Smalls had finally agreed to let me get close to her daughter, but I hadn't been able to get more out of her since the little she gave me the day before. Still, I believed I was going to be able to.

Today is a new day.

I sipped my Starbucks coffee that I bought on the way to the hospital as I walked down the hallway when suddenly I stopped in my tracks. A smile met me by the elevator, one that made my heart pound.

He approached me with his messenger bag slung over his shoulder. I wondered if it was the same bag that he had been carrying around twelve years ago when I first met him during a case back in DC, my very first case as an FBI profiler. It looked the same. And so did he.

Yet more handsome than ever.

I had liked him back then but also found him very annoying and pushy. I had ended up naming my son the same name as him because I liked his name. That's what I told myself. Now, I wondered if it was also because I liked him so much.

Not that he could ever know.

"Eva Rae Thomas!"

"Alex Huxley?"

He threw out his arms. "The one and only."

"What are you doing here?" I asked and sipped my coffee. He gave me a look, and I exhaled. "Please, no. Don't tell me you're covering this case? My case?"

He smiled again and nodded.

"Well..."

I pressed the elevator button and grumbled. "Oh, geez."

"It's been a while," he said. "I was surprised to see that you were on this case. I thought you quit? Something about a divorce, rumor has it?"

I pressed the elevator button again like I thought that would make it come faster. "If you must know, yes. Chad and I divorced. I moved to Florida. End of story."

He nodded. "Okay, none of my business. I get it."

"So, why is the *Washington Post* interested in this case?" I asked as the elevator dinged and the doors slid open.

"Why wouldn't we be? A girl comes back after fourteen years?"

"Still. It's a little much to send someone down here to report on it; I'd say," I said as I pressed the button for the fourth floor and watched as the doors closed. I turned to look at him, scrutinizing him. I guessed that he had somehow heard that we were asking questions in the DC area—probably from a source in the local police. Alex was known to have sources everywhere. It annoyed me greatly when I worked as an agent in DC because he always covered my cases, and I kept running into him everywhere I went. It often felt like he was one step ahead of me, and I never figured out how he managed that—how he always knew what was going on.

"What I wonder is why they pulled you in on this," he said, breaking the silence between us. "What's the urgency?"

I cleared my throat and looked at my sneakers. I couldn't tell him that we believed the baby taken recently was taken by the same guy who had taken Clarissa fourteen years ago. Then the elevator dinged, and the doors slid open.

"You know I'll figure it out somehow, don't you?" he yelled after me with a grin as I rushed toward Sheriff Dawson, who was waiting for me.

Chapter 16

"THIS IS A NIGHTMARE."

Linda hid her face between her hands. Her sister, Emma, put her arm around her shoulder and pulled her into a hug while Linda cried. Emma lived in South Florida, in Ft. Lauderdale, but had driven up the night before when Linda called her on the verge of tears and told her that Clarissa had come back. Linda had stayed the night at the hospital, sleeping in a chair outside Clarissa's room since the child didn't want her inside the room.

"My own daughter won't recognize that I am her mother! I've waited fourteen years for this moment—fourteen years of worrying and hoping to see her again. And this is what I get? She doesn't even want me in there. She won't talk to me and hardly even looks at me."

"I'm sorry," her sister said and rubbed her back gently. "It's awful."

Linda wiped a tear from her cheek with the palm of her hand. "I don't know what to do."

"What do the doctors say?" Emma asked. "Is this normal? Will it go away? Will she realize you are her mother eventually?"

Linda shook her head. "The doctors don't know anything. The only people who are more clueless than them are the police. They can't even figure out where she has been. I want that bastard found and prosecuted. I want him to get the freaking chair for what he did to me and my baby girl."

"That's understandable. I think we all want him to fry."

Linda sniffled, feeling the anger rise in her. "That's the only reason I let that FBI woman into Clarissa's room. I'm not happy to have her here, and just seeing her makes me want to scream. But right now, I just want that bastard found."

Linda looked at Emma. "Why won't my baby talk to me?"

"I'm sure it'll get better. She might be in shock. Maybe if she goes to therapy? Don't you think she'll eventually realize that the man who took her was a monster and a criminal?"

Linda wiped away more tears and sniffled. She lifted her head as she heard the elevator ding and saw Eva Rae Thomas step out of it, rushing toward the sheriff, carrying Starbucks coffee in her right hand. Everything about her rubbed Linda the wrong way—even the way she walked, almost waddling because she was overweight.

She watched the sheriff and Eva Rae Thomas talk for a little while, then began wondering if there was anything she was missing out on. She knew another baby had been taken, and she felt for the mother; she really did, but to her, it was personal. She wanted the guy to suffer and be punished for what he had done to her. To think that she had gotten her daughter back, yet she hadn't at all.

"Gosh, that makes me so angry. The way he messed with her mind," she said, clenching a fist. "Turning her against me, against her real mother."

Emma put a hand on her shoulder. "I'm sure they'll find him. And I'm sure that Clarissa will come back to you. You just need to give it time."

Linda knew her sister was right, but it hurt to admit it. Linda didn't believe any of these people were capable of finding this guy.

It was like what her own mother had always said: *If you want something done, then do it yourself.*

Chapter 17

THEN:

"Why are you asking me all these questions? Shouldn't you be out looking for baby Anna instead?"

Detective Brent looked down at Ron, the baby's father. They were sitting in the couple's living room and had gone over the night and the day before several times. There were a few inconsistencies in Ron's explanation, which made Brent suspicious. Meanwhile, Garcia sat with the wife in the kitchen, comforting her.

"We are. We have search teams out there," he said. "Don't worry about that part. We are doing everything we can. Your wife is a colleague. Believe me; every cop in the area is looking for your baby right now."

Brent paused, then looked at the guy in front of him. He looked tired, which was good. Maybe he would finally break down and tell the truth if he kept pressuring him. Brent had seen many cases like this, and he knew to listen to a hunch when he had one.

"Let's go over this one more time. Tell me where you were yesterday, beginning from when you woke up in the morning."

Ron groaned and rubbed the bridge of his nose. "You've got to be kidding me. I've told you this a hundred times."

"I just need it one more time," Brent said. "To make sure we didn't miss anything important."

"Like what? It was a day like all others. I went to work and came home late."

"When leaving the house in the morning, did you see anything? Any suspicious activity? Maybe a car parked outside your house? Someone standing on the sidewalk, looking like they didn't belong? Have you seen anyone watching your house these past few days?"

Ron sighed and shook his head. "I...I haven't noticed, no."

"I can't stop thinking about the fact that there is no sign of forced entry, nor have we found any fingerprints or footprints that don't belong to either of you two. How do you want to explain that?"

"I told you this," he sighed. "My wife forgot to lock the back door when she went to bed. Someone must have come in that way."

"You said that, but it's just so hard for me to comprehend. Your wife is a cop. She must know how important it is to lock the doors at night. As cops, we say this to people all the time. Lock your doors. Don't leave your keys in the car. Don't hide the keys under the doormat or in the plant next to the door—stupid stuff that people do. We repeat it every day. Can you explain to me how she —of all the people in the world—could forget something that important?"

"How am I supposed to know?" he said and threw out his arms. "You have to ask her."

"And then there's the question of how on earth this intruder, or kidnapper, knew that she forgot to lock it? It puzzles me that he would know she didn't do it when she usually always remembers. Do you see my point?"

Ron rose from his chair and gesticulated widely with his arms. "I just want my baby back. Please. Do you understand that? Do you understand ANYTHING?"

He yelled the last word, which made all chatter and activity in the house come to an immediate halt. All eyes were on him now, and one of the officers put his hand on the grip of his gun in the holster. Seeing this, Ron clenched his fists in anger yet pulled back.

"I didn't mean to…."

"There's no need to get aggressive here," Brent said and exchanged a look with Garcia, who had come to the living room. He nodded when Garcia signaled that he was okay, then mouthed with his back turned to Ron.

I think I'm onto something here.

Chapter 18

I BOUGHT another coffee on the way as I drove back toward the barrier islands. I took a left turn on 520 and continued north on A1A toward Cape Canaveral. Sierra Holmes lived with her mother in a small canal-front house from the sixties. It had recently been renovated, and I could tell they had gotten a new roof as I got out and wondered if that was because of a hurricane. Lots of people had new fences and roofs, especially after Hurricane Irma raged through our area a few years ago.

I walked up to the front porch and found the doorbell. A dog barked behind the door, and someone shushed it. Then the door opened, and a small woman looked at me through the screen. She was very muscular and obviously someone who worked out.

"Yes?"

I showed her my badge. "Eva Rae Thomas, FBI. I'm here to talk to Sierra? I called earlier."

The woman nodded. "Yes, yes, come on in." She pushed open the screen door while holding back the dog. It growled at me as I passed.

"You'll have to excuse Roger here. We just got him a few days ago to feel safer after...well, you know."

I nodded. "For protection. I get it."

"After something like this, you stop trusting people, you know?" she said. "I look at our neighbors differently, wondering if they have taken my granddaughter or if they're going to hurt me or any of my children. It's terrible. Anyway, Sierra is in the kitchen, waiting for you. I'll just take Roger to his crate."

"I appreciate it," I said and continued to the kitchen, where a young girl sat by the table, drinking a soda. She barely looked up at me as I entered, and I could read the grief on her face immediately.

"Sierra? I'm Agent Eva Rae Thomas. I called earlier?"

She nodded, and I sat down across from her. Roger started to bark from the other room, and I assumed he wasn't completely satisfied with being locked inside his crate again.

"Can I get you anything?" Sierra asked. "Water? Coffee? A soda?"

I shook my head and smiled softly. "I'm fine, but thanks."

I opened the folder I had gotten from the sheriff earlier and read through it before leaving the hospital. He had also briefed me on what they knew and had worked on so far, which wasn't impressive, if I was honest. The young girl in front of me was no more than sixteen years old—the same age as my oldest daughter. I had to take a deep breath to focus on why I was there. I just wanted to hug the poor girl and tell her it would be okay. What she was going through had to be beyond awful.

"Do you have any news? Do you know who took my baby?" she asked with a sniffle.

I forced a smile. "We're doing everything we can."

"Why does everyone keep saying that?" she asked. "Is that something they teach you to say?"

That made me smile. "I guess you have heard that a lot, huh?"

"Constantly. It doesn't really help me, though."

"Of course not. You know what? I'll level with you. No, we don't have a lot of leads, but we are following the few we have. We do believe your baby was taken by the same guy who took a baby fourteen years ago. The girl just returned, and we are trying to figure out where she has been. We do believe that she was kept out of the state, and we're following that trail. Does that help a little?"

Sierra frowned. "I just don't understand…you say the same guy?"

I nodded. "Yes."

"But…I've already told you that it was a woman who took my baby. She was a nurse, and she took Desiree to have some tests done, and then I never saw her again."

I nodded. "I know. That's why I'm here. How certain are you that it was a woman? It says in the file that you didn't get a good look at her face?"

Sierra became pensive for a few seconds. Then, she shook her head. "I don't know anymore. It's all such a blur. I barely remember what Desiree looks like. I only had her for a few hours. I don't even remember what it felt like to hold her."

She paused to cry and hid her face between her hands. It was devastating to watch.

"Did you take any photos of her?" I asked, hiding how my voice was cracking. This girl could be my Olivia. I couldn't even imagine the pain she had to feel. "With your phone?"

She nodded with a sniffle. "I keep staring at them, so I don't forget her. I gave them to the officers when they did the Amber Alert and sent her picture out to all the media."

I nodded. "Of course. Could you airdrop a few for me?"

"Sure," she said and grabbed her phone. She tapped a few times, and I received the photos on my phone.

"Thanks."

Sierra went quiet, then looked up at me, her eyes big and glassy. "This girl, the one that came back. I saw the story about her in the news. She was gone for fourteen years, you say? And no one found her all that time?"

I nodded, feeling heavy. This couldn't be very reassuring to Sierra.

"And now she's back with her mother?"

"Yes. They've been reunited."

A tear escaped her eye, and she didn't wipe it away. "Does that mean I have to wait fourteen years before I see Desiree again?"

"Oh, sweetie. You can't think like that."

"This girl. They say that she's in good health, right? He must have taken good care of her?"

"True, but we don't know much about what has happened to her yet since she won't talk to us."

I swallowed, thinking about the fact that Clarissa was pregnant. I couldn't tell Sierra that. I simply couldn't.

"But the difference is that my baby needs surgery," she said. "Or she won't survive. Does the kidnapper know this?"

"It's been said over and over again in the news, but we don't know if the kidnapper watches it. We hope he will and that he will come to his senses and give her back once he realizes what is at stake."

Sierra sobbed. "I'm scared."

I took her hands in mine. "I know. It must be very scary for you."

"I just want my baby back. Why would anyone take my baby from me? How could anyone be that cruel?"

"My guess is we're looking at a very sick person," I said. "But also very intelligent. He got away with this once and thinks he can do it again. But he will make a mistake this time; I promise you. And when he does, we'll find him and get Desiree back to you."

Her eyes met mine, and suddenly there was a light in them. "There is something that I thought about right before you got here. I don't know if it's important, but I want you to know anyway."

Chapter 19

THE BABY WAS CRYING AGAIN. He didn't understand why. She had eaten and should be sleeping now, but she kept wailing like something was wrong, and it filled him with great unease.

"What's wrong, little Sandra?"

He stared at her in the crib, then wondered if he should pick her up, but he didn't want her to think that every time she started to cry, he would do that. He wanted her to learn how to sleep when she was put in the crib.

"Shh, shh, little baby," he whispered. "You need to sleep now."

The baby's face was red and seemed torn. It broke his heart to see it. "What's going on, little baby? Huh?"

He reached inside the crib and caressed her gently across her head, trying to calm her without picking her up. "Shhhh. Please, just sleep now. You're so tired. You need to nap."

He took a deep breath as the baby seemed to calm slightly, and he removed his hand. Sandra's small eyelids slid shut, and she stopped wailing. He smiled when seeing this, and his shoulders came down.

"Finally," he whispered, then stepped back cautiously so as not to make a sound. He walked out of the nursery and turned on the baby monitor, then snuck downstairs into the kitchen, where he sat down in a chair, feeling exhausted. He had forgotten how tough it was having an infant. But he also knew that it was going to get better. The first few years with Cate had been hard too, but also amazing. There was nothing like becoming a father. It would all pay off later.

Nothing was more rewarding.

He grabbed a cup of coffee from the pot and sat back down to drink it. He stared at his phone. He had gotten a notification but didn't pick it up. He had cut himself off from social media and didn't follow the news. He didn't want to have anything to do with the world outside. Right now, it was just him and Sandra, and he didn't need anything or anyone else. She was all there was.

He sighed and sipped his coffee when he heard a sound from the monitor. He looked at the screen, feeling weary. Sandra had only slept ten minutes, and that definitely wasn't enough. She'd be cranky if she didn't get more sleep than that.

Please sleep a little longer, baby.

He stared at the screen and saw no movement. There was no more noise. It was just a false alarm. She was still asleep.

He breathed, relieved, and let go of the monitor. He walked to the window and looked out into the yard. The trees were covered with heavy snow. It had been coming down for days now, and it looked beautiful outside.

Another noise came from the monitor. His heart dropped.

He stared at the screen, then realized she was moving.

She was awake.

And then the crying came back. Louder than earlier.

Louder than ever.

Chapter 20

I FELT COMPLETELY DRAINED when I drove up DeLeon Road and spotted my house at almost the end of it. My neighbors had just bought a new boat and were trying to park it in the driveway, and while doing so, they were blocking the street with their trailer. It was a gorgeous boat, one that I was sure they'd have tons of fun in. They liked to go fishing off the shore, and the husband, Liam, always had to show me pictures of the fish he had caught. Many of them were small sharks.

I waved at Liam and his wife as they thanked me for my patience while getting the boat into the driveway.

I didn't see him until I was already out of the car. I felt my heart drop. Not because he looked so amazing—which he totally did—but more because I knew seeing him meant trouble. He was sitting outside my porch swing, which I had recently bought and set up myself. I wasn't much of a handywoman, so that was a proud moment in my life. One I had hoped my daughters would think of as cool as well, but they hadn't been very interested when I showed them what I had accomplished.

Alexander Huxley didn't even get up as I approached the porch with the keys dangling in my hand.

"Nice swing," he said with a grin, then moved it back and forth with his legs. It squeaked annoyingly.

"Alex, what are you doing here?" I sighed deeply. "How do you even know where I live?"

He tilted his head. "I never reveal my…."

"Sources, yes, you've said that before."

I looked at the take-out I had in my hand from my favorite Thai place downtown. It smelled heavenly still, and I didn't want it to go cold. I had the night off from my youngest and had planned to eat, then sleep, and nothing else.

"Can I come in?" he asked.

I shook my head. "Why? I don't have anything for you. There is no news, so no story."

I put the key in the lock, and he got up and walked to me. "I'm not quite sure about that."

I closed my eyes briefly. I could still smell the food in my hand. I had bought enough for the kids and me but could eat it all myself. I was that hungry.

"Now, exactly what do you mean by that?" I asked tiredly. I wasn't in the mood for his games, no matter how charming he was while baiting me.

Alex ran a hand through his thick hair. He looked like he just stepped out of a commercial for after-shave. It annoyed me.

"Let me in, and I'll tell you what my next story is going to be about." He looked down at the bag in my hand. "Is that Thai? I absolutely love Thai food."

I stared at him, barely blinking. Was this guy for real? Did he seriously expect me to invite him in for dinner with my children?

"I'll give you the address of the place, and you can go get your own food."

He smiled again. I found him both annoyingly repulsive and

extremely attractive. It was so frustrating. I wanted to kiss him and punch him at the same time.

"Now, if you'll excuse me, I have to eat dinner with my family," I said and opened the door. He placed a hand above mine on the handle. I froze at the touch and felt a warmth spread. I lifted my gaze and met his.

"It's the same, right?"

He kept looking into my eyes as he spoke.

"W-what is?"

I sounded insecure and nervous; it drove me nuts. Why did he make me so flustered? I was a forty-three-year-old woman for crying out loud. I had four children. Nothing should make me flustered anymore, especially not some guy with a handsome smile.

"The person who took the baby," he said. "It's the same person who took that girl who came back, Clarissa. Am I right?"

I stared into his eyes, my throat growing tight. I had never been a good liar, and especially not to him. I removed my gaze and looked ahead, then shook my head. "I can't comment on that."

He let go of my hand and pulled back. "Okay. But that will be my story in tomorrow's newspaper."

He paused for effect, then leaned close to my ear.

"You'll probably need to practice that poker face of yours for when the rest of the media throws themselves at you because it's not working for you as it is right now. Good night. Enjoy your food. It smells heavenly."

Chapter 21

"PREGNANT? You're telling me my child is...?"

Linda Smalls stared at Sheriff Dawson, who was standing in front of her. She wasn't blinking and was barely breathing. It was like the bad news just kept coming at her like an endless heavy freight train. It refused to stop, just kept going, kept running over her.

Ka-chunk, ka-chunk, ka-chunk.

Sheriff Dawson rubbed his forehead. He barely looked at her when he spoke. It was strange, and it seemed like he was guilty of something to her.

"I...I'm afraid so, ma'am."

Linda looked for a chair. She had to sit down. Her sister came up to her. She had stayed with her all day and said she'd stay for as long as necessary. Linda couldn't catch her breath. Her chest felt constricted and tight. She had known that there was a possibility that her child had been mistreated and molested and maybe even raped since she had been in captivity for fourteen years and whoever took her had to be the worst scum of this earth. She had actually prepared for that fact and even talked to a therapist about it. But nothing could prepare her for the day when she got the news—when it hit her.

Nothing.

"We have a psychologist you can talk to...ma'am, if...."

She lifted her gaze and met his. "A psychologist? I'm not the one who needs help here. In there, behind that door, is my daughter, who has barely gone through puberty. She is carrying a child—a child as a result of rape, maybe even several years of abuse, and she doesn't even know her real mother. What kind of a creature would do this to a child? Tell me who?"

"That is what we're trying to figure out and why we have involved a profiler," he said, almost mumbling. It was obvious he felt very uncomfortable, and he was almost stepping on his own toes. He was a joke, Linda thought to herself. A cliché.

Useless.

"I don't need to talk to your psychologist," she snorted at him. "Just find whoever did this to my child, and do it fast! I want him to fry."

Dawson nodded, holding his hat between his hands. "Y-yes, ma'am, we're working on it. We're putting all our resources into this case. Rest assured."

"Oh, there will be no assured rest for me till this bastard has paid."

Linda felt her sister's hand on her arm, trying to calm her down. But she couldn't ease up. This was simply the last drop. She couldn't hold the tears back anymore.

"We need your permission to take a DNA sample from the baby," he said. "To determine who is the father."

Linda wrinkled her forehead. "Well, of course, you have my permission. Go and do whatever it takes."

"Thank you, ma'am," the sheriff said. He nodded nervously, then turned around on his heel and disappeared down the hallway of the hospital. Linda stared at the door to Clarissa's room. She had tried to go in there earlier and talk to her, but her daughter wouldn't even look at her. She just stared at the window, lying on her side, her back turned toward Linda. It broke her heart, and now that she had received this news, that her kid had been sexually abused, well, it just added to her anger. She looked at her sister, who smiled comfortingly, tilting her head slightly in pity. Linda clenched her fists as hard as she could.

Someone had to pay for this. And soon.

Chapter 22

MY MOOD WAS low for pretty much the rest of the evening. I ate with the kids, trying to forget what Alexander Huxley had told me. I really didn't want the public to know that we believed it was the same kidnapper. And I didn't want our kidnapper to know either since that would only make him act more carefully. I needed him out of hiding and hoped he would make a mistake soon.

"Mom, I'm gonna need clothes for prom," Olivia said.

Behind her, the TV was turned on to CNN.

I looked away from the screen and into her eyes. She had just gotten a new haircut that was even shorter than earlier. It looked cute, but I didn't want her to go any shorter. She wasn't wearing any make-up like her friends did, and I liked that. They all looked like small dolls, and I even saw them on social media sometimes in tiny outfits that made my skin crawl, making duck lips, and wearing a lot of make-up. I was so happy my girl wasn't like them. She was more into gaming and music and often just wore baggy pants and a hoodie, even on warm days in Florida.

I smiled. "Okay, so let's try and go dress shopping this week."

Olivia blushed and looked down. "Could I maybe just get the money and buy something myself?"

That made my heart drop. "I'm not fun enough to go shopping with anymore? Am I that embarrassing?"

Olivia growled and dropped her fork. "Argh. Why do you have to make it about you?"

Christine stopped chewing and looked at her sister. Alex barely noticed what was going on and gobbled down his fried rice and chicken so fast I feared he would choke. I always wondered what the rush was with the boy since he seemed always to be in a hurry. It was a problem in school, too, that he refused to sit still. But he got bored so easily. They said it was because he was gifted, and school was too easy for him. I had hoped that playing soccer would help drain some of that energy, but now he was suspended from the team.

He finished his plate, then ran from the table, almost forgetting to take out his plate but remembering it at the last second.

"I'm sorry," I said, addressed to Olivia. "I didn't mean to make it about me. I was just disappointed. I was looking forward to having a girl's day out shopping with my daughter. I have wanted to go dress shopping for prom with you since you were very young."

Olivia rolled her eyes at me and groaned. "You're making way too big of a deal out of this. As always. Can't you just give me money and I'll buy something myself? It's not that big of a deal."

I chewed. "Of course. If that's how you want it."

"And now you're acting all disappointed! I really just want to go on my own. You don't have to make it about you."

I lifted my hands resignedly. "I'm trying not to. But you can't tell me not to be sad when it was something I was looking forward to."

"I knew you'd make a big deal out of it. You're so annoying."

Olivia stood to her feet and pushed the chair out behind her. She groaned, annoyed, then started to walk away. I stopped her.

"Don't forget to take out your plate, please."

Olivia grumbled again, grabbed her plate, and took it to the kitchen. I looked at Christine and shook my head while listening to her clang and bang aggressively with the plate and silverware as she put it in the dishwasher.

"Don't look at me," Christine said. "I don't think you handled that very well. It was very insensitive. You really should think a little more before you speak."

She emptied her glass of water and rose to her feet, carrying out her own plate to the kitchen. I stared after her, not knowing exactly when those two girls had become best friends. They used to fight about everything. I shrugged and turned up the volume on the TV, so I wouldn't feel so alone when everyone had left.

They were reporting live from a press conference with Kansas Senator Hartnett, who talked about her pregnancy. She was giving birth in six weeks but promised that she would, of course, perform her duties as a member of Congress as close to her due date as possible. She was smiling happily from ear to ear and caressing her bulging stomach as the reporters asked their questions, and it warmed my heart. They asked her if her age would be a problem since she was in her forties, and that made me annoyed at them. I had given birth to my youngest child while in my forties and had no problems. It was a silly question, in my opinion. Hartnett answered them that the doctors assured her she was in perfectly good shape to have her baby, and so far, the pregnancy had passed by with no problems.

"You tell them, girl," I said and started to clean up after dinner, still smiling happily for her.

There was nothing like the prospect of a new baby being born to make me feel excited. And then I was overwhelmed with sadness. I realized that I missed Angel, who was at her father's. It was such a double-edged sword being separated. On the one hand,

I really enjoyed it when she was at his place because it gave me time to be with my other children and actually pay attention to them. But at the same time, I missed that little Curly Sue so much it felt like it would kill me.

Trying to think of something else while I filled the dishwasher, I returned to my visit with Sierra earlier. She had told me she still couldn't remember the kidnapper's face, as the memory was too blurry, but there had been a bracelet that she remembered vividly because she noticed it when this person took her baby from her to get the tests done. The bracelet had braided leather straps and a copper piece on top of the arm with a rising red sun etched into it. Sierra said she kept dreaming about it at night, and it wasn't till recently that she realized it had been on the hand of the person taking her baby. She had made a drawing for me, and now I took it out and stared at it, wondering where the heck one got a bracelet like this. Who would know if this was a common piece of jewelry? If we showed it to the media to ask the public, we would probably get thousands of people calling in knowing of someone who had one that was similar. Or was it just unique enough to point us to him?

I sighed and put the drawing away. The senator thanked the press and was about to leave when a reporter asked her why she had waited so long to tell the world—if it had anything to do with what happened last time she had a child.

The senator ignored the question and left the conference, but I couldn't help noticing that she suddenly seemed a little out of it. I wondered if she had miscarried and if they had tried for years to get pregnant again. Then I thought about Linda and how hard it had to be for her to continue living after Clarissa went missing. She had an eight-year-old now, so it had taken her six years before she had another. I didn't like the woman, yet I couldn't help feeling sorry for her. So much pain she had to go through and getting

Clarissa back had only added to it. The very thing she had been praying for and hoping to happen had turned out to be a complete nightmare. And now, figuring out that her daughter was pregnant at only fourteen?

It had to be profoundly devastating. I couldn't even imagine.

Chapter 23

THEN:

They interviewed them both for hours on end, and then they finally allowed Ron back in the kitchen with Amelia. She looked up at him with tears in her eyes, and he grabbed her hands in his. Detectives Brent and Garcia watched them. Brent was even more convinced that something was fishy about the dad than ever.

Brent nodded at Garcia, signaling for him to walk with him outside, where he lit a cigarette.

"I have a theory," he said, blowing out smoke. "But so far, it's just between you and me."

Garcia nodded. He looked up to Brent and always clung to every word he said. Brent liked that about the colleague. He didn't think he already knew everything like most kids these days. They had no respect for those of them who had been doing this for many years and who had the experience. But not Garcia. He respected Brent more than anyone, and Brent enjoyed that very much. Garcia was a smart guy, and Brent didn't think twice before sharing his wisdom with him.

"I say the dad is hiding something."

"Really?"

"I'm positive."

He smoked again and paused for effect. "My guess is he got frustrated with the kid and did something to her. I've seen it before. Lack of sleep can drive people crazy. And those infants are so fragile right after birth. He might have shaken her a little too hard because she was crying in the middle of the night. You know."

Garcia's eyes grew big and wide as he stared at his colleague. "Really? I...I didn't...the mom didn't seem to know anything."

Brent smoked again and looked out into the street. The spectators that had gathered outside of the tape earlier had disappeared. News was only new for so long before it got old. People moved on, minding their own business. Soon, it would be nothing but a story people told each other at dinner parties.

Did you hear what happened to the neighbors?

"My guess is he didn't tell her. He probably got rid of the body in the middle of the night. Buried her in the back or something."

"Wow," Garcia said, barely noticing that Brent blew smoke in his face. "I...I can't believe...."

"Yeah, it happened down south a few years ago when we were on a case down there—me and Gibson, my old partner. The dad killed the poor kid in a fit of rage because he wouldn't stop crying. It turned out the dad had taken the kid to a lake and dumped him. But in that case, the mom saw it happen, and he threatened to kill her if she said anything. She finally broke down and told us everything after ten hours of interrogation—ugly case. I'll never forget the desperation in her eyes as she finally caved in. Can you imagine having to cover for the man who killed your child? There are some real scumbags out there, I tell ya.'"

"What do we do next?"

Garcia had barely finished his sentence when the dad, Ron, came out on the porch to them. Brent threw away his cigarette and looked at him. Ron seemed upset.

"Can you guys come back in for a minute? My wife suddenly remembered something that might be useful," he said.

"Oh, she did now, did she?" Brent said, lifting an eyebrow.

Or did you just feed her a story to tell, threatening to kill her if she didn't? I'm onto you, you bastard. I'm not letting you get away with this. I'm not making the same mistake twice.

"Yes, there is someone from her past who might want to hurt us. Come in; she'll tell you everything."

Part III
WASHINGTON, DC

Two days later

Chapter 24

IT WAS late in the afternoon when I landed at Dulles. I grabbed my weekend bag from the overhead compartment. I had packed it so fast that I had barely any idea what was in it. I was only going to stay for a few nights, so I had to get by with whatever I had grabbed while rushing out the door.

Luckily, my mom had been able to come and stay with the kids, while Matt agreed to keep Angel for a couple more days.

Not that he was happy about it. He had plans, he said. But he wouldn't tell me what was so important that he couldn't keep his daughter. It was apparently none of my business.

"Well, whatever your plans are, they'll either have to involve your daughter or wait until I get back," I said.

As I reached the airport's exit doors, I spotted a black-haired woman in a button-up shirt and black pants with a sign and my name on it. She smiled as I approached her. She had a beautiful smile.

"Agent Thomas?"

I nodded. She reached out her hand. "Agent Walsh. It's an

honor to meet you. I have read all your books and am a great admirer of your work."

She spoke with an accent and almost sang as the words flowed out of her. She was beyond gorgeous.

"I'll be your ride."

I followed her to a black SUV and got in. She started the car, and it felt like we almost soared out of the parking lot.

"I hear you've located the Baby-Snatcher?"

I stared at her. "Is that what you're calling him now?"

She smiled. "It was what they called him in an article in the *Post*. It caught on.'"

"Let me guess," I said with an exhale. "Alexander Huxley."

"You know him?"

"You might say that. I know his way of sensationalizing everything."

Walsh nodded. "Yeah, but it's quite catchy, right? You gotta give him that."

"If I must."

Walsh smiled again. Her short black hair was shaved on the sides, making her look tough, yet her smile was soft and mild.

"They said something about some DNA evidence that led you here?" she asked.

I nodded. "He was previously known."

"And the bastard got her pregnant?" Walsh took a turn and shook her head in disbelief. "The agony she must have been through. Poor kid."

"You can say that again," I said with a sigh, thinking of Clarissa.

The DNA results taken from her unborn baby had come a day ago, and then when it was run in the federal system as I insisted that it be because I had a feeling she was kept out of state, a match had come up in my old hometown, DC. It fit well with the fact that she was wearing a necklace with the emblem from the local boxing club, which wasn't situated far from the address that came up in the system under the name. The owners of the boxing club had recognized her and said she'd come in with her dad once a week, always paid cash, but they didn't know their address. They also said she stopped coming about six months ago, and they believed they had moved.

The local police in DC had done all the work in finding this guy. He had been arrested seventeen years ago for a rape he was later acquitted for, but his DNA had been stored in the system. Luckily for us, someone had done their job properly, and now we were going to get the sick bastard. We hoped he still had baby Desiree and that she was still alive.

I had come to take them both with me back to Florida. Hopefully, it all ended here.

Chapter 25

BABY SANDRA HAD BEEN SLEEPING without waking up for two entire days, and it was driving him crazy. It was good that she wasn't crying, but the sleeping worried him even more. He tried to wake her up to feed her, but she wouldn't take the bottle. Now, he stared at her, feeling the anxiety rush through him.

What do I do?

"Just wake up, will you? Please, wake up."

He moaned in agony, not knowing how to deal with this. He picked her up and tried to bounce her back and forth as he had tried so many times before, but the infant remained limp between his hands. He had grown to miss the incessant crying. There was nothing good about a quiet baby.

"What is wrong with you, little sweetheart?" he asked as he had asked so many times before, but this time he was on the verge of breaking down. This was more than he could handle. What was wrong with her? Sleeping a lot was normal; he remembered that from Cate, but they usually woke up at some point. They would get hungry, right? But this baby just seemed not to want to eat. She hadn't grown at all, and suddenly her legs seemed swollen.

He stared at her small legs and then noticed her face was swollen as well. Also, her breathing had become labored.

This can't be good.

Panic started to erupt inside him as he bounced back and forth, trying to wake her.

"Come on, little baby. Please, open your eyes for me, will you?"

And then a minor miracle happened. She actually opened then. For the first time in two days, she opened her eyelids and looked directly at him, then made a slight squeaking sound.

"There you are," he said with great relief. He grabbed the bottle and placed it on her lips. Her tiny body barely moved, and he pressed the bottle in between her lips, frantically trying to feed her.

"Come on, baby. You must be hungry. You gotta eat so you can grow and become big and fat like all the other babies, right?"

Please.

He was almost crying now when Sandra finally latched onto the bottle and took a couple of sips. He gasped with relief as she ate a little more.

"There you go, little baby. There you go. You can do it," he said while bouncing her. Her small blue eyes stared at him while she feebly managed to get the milk inside of her tiny body that felt like it had only gotten smaller since the day before.

Sandra's eyelids became heavy, and she stopped sucking.

"No, no," he said. "Keep eating so you can grow, sweetie. Don't fall back asleep, please."

He walked to the window so she could look outside and maybe get some light to keep her awake. As a ray of sunlight hit her face, she blinked her eyes and woke up again, then took another sip of the bottle. She blinked a few times, then dozed off again.

"All right," he said. "I guess we'll have to take small steps, huh? Baby steps…heh. At least you got a little nourishment inside you. That will have to do for now."

He bounced her a little more while looking out onto the street. It was a beautiful day out, and he wished he could take her for a walk in the stroller. But it was still too early. He would have to wait a little longer in case someone saw them. It was probably too cold anyway. Sandra would be freezing, and he couldn't risk that.

"We'll get out there in time for spring, won't we, baby Sandra?"

He was about to turn and put her down for her nap when he heard the sirens and peeked out the window just in time to see an invasion of black cars swarm into his street.

Chapter 26

WE HAD GONE through a short briefing with the DC police before moving out with their SWAT team. I was sitting in the car with Walsh, following the cars rushing down the street with the long rows of townhouses. The first one drove up in front of the address and parked, and the rest of us followed shortly after. We were all dressed in Kevlar vests and armed. The DC police officers rushed to the front door first. I got out and waited for a clear signal. There was yelling coming from inside, and a woman screamed.

Then the signal came, and I walked closer with Walsh following on my tail. I entered the house, wearing my FBI jacket. Inside the kitchen, I saw a woman lying on her stomach, hands behind her back as she was being detained. I scanned the room to see if I could spot any baby or hear any crying other than what came from the woman.

"Is that all?" I asked as I was approached by the SWAT team commander, John Rivers.

He nodded. "We're still searching upstairs. But so far, no baby, and no sign of our suspect, Steve Melton."

I walked to the woman on the floor and knelt next to her.

"Where is Steve?"

"I...I don't know," she said, her voice shaking. "I was just making dinner, and then...suddenly...."

She was in deep shock. Her eyes were fearful, and she was speaking through heavy sobs. Next to her on the floor was a plate shattered on the tiles, and taco shells were scattered all over the floor. She wasn't lying to me. At least not about that part.

"What's your name?"

"D-Dana."

"Okay, Dana. We're looking for Steve Melton. Where is he?" I asked. "I assume he is your husband? Or boyfriend?"

She nodded, closing her eyes briefly like she was running out of strength. "My husband."

"We need to find him quickly. Do you know where he is?"

"He...he was here. But then he left. He ran out the back door," she said.

"He must have seen us coming down the street," I said, signaling Walsh to alert the others to start a search of the area. She left right away. "He won't make it far."

"W-why...what's happening?" Dana asked.

"I'm looking for the baby, Dana. It's very important that we find her. Did he take her with him when he ran?"

Dana looked up at me, straining her neck.

"B-baby?"

"Think about this very carefully, Dana. Right now, you can choose. You help me, and I'll help you stay out of prison, okay?"

"Prison? I don't...understand."

"The baby, Dana. Where is she?"

She shook her head and sobbed.

"I don't know."

"Come on, Dana. Do you really want to go down as his accomplice? I don't think you want to do that. Just tell me if he took her with him or if she is somewhere in this house. It's very important.

Her life is in danger if she isn't taken to a hospital soon. She needs surgery."

She looked at me like she didn't believe me.

"Surgery? I don't understand."

"The baby isn't here," Rivers said, entering the kitchen behind me.

"We must assume he took her when he ran," I said and got up. I signaled to two officers. "Take her in while we search the area for her husband and the baby. They can't have gotten far."

Chapter 27

WE TURNED into a street behind the townhouse. Walsh was at the wheel while I kept an eye on our surroundings. We had ten cars out searching for this guy right now, scanning through the entire neighborhood. There was no way he could get away. It was only a matter of time.

I just prayed that it wasn't too late.

I looked down at the picture of him on my phone. It was the same one that had been sent out to the entire search team. It was the picture taken when Steve Melton was arrested seventeen years ago. It probably didn't look much like him anymore. I wished I had a more current photo of him and wondered if we shouldn't just find him on social media. There had to be better pictures somewhere? But then again, if he had the baby with him, I figured he wouldn't be hard to recognize.

"Who is that?"

I pointed, and Walsh turned her head.

"Over there. A guy with a stroller. Let's go."

She floored the SUV, and we jerked forward. We reached the guy, and I jumped out, hand resting on my gun in the holster. The man stopped walking and looked at us, baffled. He was wearing a long coat and boots to better walk in the snow. It was cold out, and the wind felt freezing on my cheeks, yet the adrenaline rushing through my body kept me warm enough.

"Stop," I yelled. "Hands where I can see them."

He lifted both his hands. I stared at his face, unsure if this was him or not. "Steve Melton?"

He wrinkled his forehead.

"N-no."

I glanced at the baby in the stroller. It was a boy and probably about Angel's age, a little less than a year. I released the hand from the grip of my gun and eased up.

"It's not him," I said and signaled Walsh to step down. "I'm sorry, sir. We're looking for a man with a baby, and you fit the profile. I'm truly sorry if we frightened you. Have you by chance seen this man?"

I showed him my phone, and he looked at the picture. "That's the guy in 225B," he said and pointed toward the house. "I don't know his name, but I have seen him from time to time. I haven't lived here very long. My wife and I moved here recently with our two children. It was supposed to be a nice neighborhood and safe to raise children. That's what we were told."

"But you haven't seen him around within the past few minutes?" I asked. "While walking in the area? Maybe he passed you?"

He looked at me, puzzled. "No, I haven't."

"Is there anywhere he might be able to hide around here?" I asked, thinking he would need to get the baby inside as soon as possible. She wouldn't survive out in the cold in her condition.

"Any abandoned houses? Or houses for sale?"

"Sure. Down at the end of this street, there's a house that has been for sale forever. I don't really understand why no one has bought it yet. It's quite nice. They probably priced it too high, if you ask me. I don't know if the owners still live in it or not. I haven't seen any activity down there for a while."

"Let's go check it out," Walsh said and walked toward the SUV. I thanked the man and followed her, jumping into the car just as she took off.

Chapter 28

HE FOUND the entrance to the attic inside the walk-in closet and pulled down the ladder. With baby Sandra in his arms, still sleeping heavily, he crawled up and then pulled the hitch shut after him. It was dirty up there, and he could feel the dust between his fingers as he crawled deeper inside, into the darkness where he couldn't be seen. Sandra was so quiet that he had to stop and make sure she was still breathing before continuing. He reached the end of the attic and couldn't go any further, then he sat down with the baby in his lap, wrapping her tightly in the blanket. Her body was so small it felt almost impossible that she was still alive. But she was still breathing, even though it was abnormally labored.

"We will make it, the two of us," he whispered to her while tears rolled down his cheeks. "We just need to wait it out. We can do that, can't we? Just the two of us. We can make it."

He wiped the tears away, then leaned his head back and put the baby up against his chest, making sure she stayed warm. He closed his eyes and tried to remain calm.

"Everything is going to be just fine. Soon. It'll all be good again. We just have to get through this."

He opened his eyes when he heard the sound of a car stopping outside. There were no windows in the attic, so he couldn't look out. Instead, he stayed completely still, trying to listen over the sound of his rapidly beating heart.

Just remain completely still, he told himself.

He heard the knocking on the front door; then someone yelled: "FBI, we're coming in." He held his breath. For once, he was happy that Sandra was being so quiet, even though he feared something was terribly wrong with her.

Don't move a muscle.

He gasped lightly when he heard steps on the stairs, and soon voices were coming from the bedroom where the entrance to the attic was. Luckily for him, the hitch was very hard to see in the ceiling of the walk-in closet. Hopefully, they wouldn't spot it.

"I'm checking the closet," a voice said, and he held his breath, hugging the baby closer to his chest.

I'll never let them take her. Never.

Noises were coming from right below him now, and voices were talking loudly. "You see any signs of a baby living here like a pacifier, a bottle, or a diaper—you let me know," one of them yelled.

"Of course," another voice replied.

There were at least two then. But he didn't hear any more, so maybe it was just them.

Please, don't see the hitch, please.

The voices went quiet, and he listened carefully, thinking that maybe they had left.

"Is there an attic in these houses?" the first voice suddenly said, startling him. He felt his heart race in his chest and caressed the baby's hair gently, deciding what he would do if they came up here. He reached into the back of his pants and pulled out the gun he had brought with him.

If they do come in, it ends here.

His hand holding the gun shook badly while he heard fumbling by the hitch. He took a deep breath, then cocked the gun and placed it on the baby's head.

I will not let them take her away from me. No one takes my daughter.

Chapter 29

THEN:

"I don't know why I didn't think of him before."

Amelia looked at Ron. He took her hand in his and squeezed it. "It's okay. You're thinking of him now. They can go look for her there."

Brent looked at them, then at Garcia, and rolled his eyes. "You're saying you dated this guy? How many years ago was it again?"

Amelia looked confused. "I think it has to be…at least five years ago, yes, because it was while I still worked at that ACE hardware store, on Fifteenth. He worked there too, and we dated for a few months."

Detective Brent wrote it down, even though he felt it was a waste of his time. "Have you seen him since?"

"Yes. That's why I thought of him. I met him while I was in the supermarket a few weeks ago." She paused to think. "It must be around three weeks ago, I think, yes. That's it."

Her husband nodded and caressed her hand. "That's good, sweetie. It's good that you remembered this."

Brent sent him a glare. The poor woman had no idea who she was sitting next to, did she?

We're wasting precious time here. We should be interrogating him instead. Take him in and grill him properly.

"And that's when he saw the baby," she continued. "Maybe he got jealous? He's always been strange, especially around kids. I just had a bad feeling about him but didn't know who to tell about it. You know when you sense that someone is capable of committing something terrible. I remember when a young girl went missing back then, and I talked to him about it. I said, 'What an awful thing to happen to such a little girl,' and then he got all distant and said in a very cold manner, almost like he was reading from a script, 'Yeah, that's awful, isn't it?' but it felt like he didn't really mean it. I remember thinking that something was off about him."

"Uh-huh," Brent said and took notes. He didn't doubt that Amelia was right about this guy—that something was off. After all, as a cop, she had received training in reading people and finding criminals, but he just wasn't sure this guy was the one who had taken her baby. "And you think he might have taken baby Anna? Why do you think he would do that?"

She looked at Ron, then down at her hands that she held folded on the table. "I sort of cheated on him with Ron here. I met him before we broke up. I don't think that Tom ever forgave me for that."

"That gives him a motive, right?" Ron asked.

Agent Garcia nodded.

"You will check him out, right?" Ron continued, looking from one to the other, searching for confirmation.

Garcia turned to look at Brent.

"We will do it right away," Garcia said. "Right?"

Brent exhaled, then leaned back in his chair. He knew he had to check this one out; it was his job to hunt down each and every lead, even if his instincts told him it was a huge waste of their resources.

He nodded in agreement, then looked at the couple. "Of course. We'll do it right away. I just need you to give me his full name and address, and we'll go have a chat with him."

"Have a chat?" Ron asked, standing to his feet. "If this guy has taken my daughter…then…you need to do a lot more than that."

He was pointing aggressively at Brent.

"Sir, I'm gonna need you to calm down for me," he said. "We're doing everything we can."

"But what if that isn't enough?" Ron asked angrily. "It's like you…It's like you're not even taking this seriously. Here, my wife is saying that…."

"Ron!"

Amelia had risen to her feet too. "These people are doing the best they can. I'm a cop, too, remember? I'm sure they're doing everything. Besides, we need to let them go now; we're wasting their time with all this."

Ron stared at her while calming himself down. He ran a hand through his hair, then nodded.

"You're right. I'm sorry. It's just so frustrating."

"It is for the both of us," Amelia said. "Not just for you. We're together in this."

Brent got up, and Garcia followed. Garcia put a hand on Ron's shoulder. "We'll go visit this guy right now, okay?"

Ron hid his face between his hands. "O-okay. Good. Thank you."

"You can thank us later," Brent said and walked toward the door, then opened it and stepped out.

Like when we handcuff you for the crime that right now you're thinking you got away with. But not on my watch. That isn't happening as long as I am on this case.

Chapter 30

"I THINK there's a hitch here. Let me just pull it."

I found a chair to stand on because I wasn't tall enough. I let my hands reach for the small handle. I grabbed it and pulled. It slipped out of my hand, but I reached up again and got another grip, then pulled. Finally, the hitch cracked open, and I could see the ladder. I got down from the chair then pulled it down toward me.

"I'm going up," I yelled at Walsh. "To the attic."

I placed a hand on the grip of my gun and took it out. I got up on the first step when Walsh came up behind me.

"I see no signs of a baby living here," she said.

"He's good at hiding his tracks; he's done it for fourteen years with Clarissa," I said and continued up the steps.

"What if it isn't the same guy?" she asked. "Have you thought about that? It might be a coincidence, or maybe someone copying him?"

I paused on the fourth step and looked down at her. "First of all, I showed Clarissa Smalls the drawing of the bracelet that had been on the arm of whoever kidnapped Sierra Holmes's baby. Even though she didn't say so, I could tell that Clarissa recognized it, which tells me the two kidnappers are the same person. Second of all, I don't believe in coincidences."

Walsh smiled. "I heard that about you."

"You shouldn't either if you want to get good at this. Just a piece of advice," I said. "Don't ever take the easy route because the killers won't. They will go to extreme lengths to try and trick you. If you sense a connection, you go with that instinct even when your colleagues and your boss all say you're crazy. Trust that gut feeling."

I tapped my stomach.

"Even when they call me crazy? Wow."

"I've been called way worse than that," I said and turned to look up at the darkness in front of me. My stomach felt strange—like something was off. I paused and stared at where I was going, then decided to continue. I took two more steps when Walsh's phone rang. She picked it up while I continued up the stairs. I reached the last one and was about to turn on my flashlight when Walsh spoke below me.

"They've seen him. Let's go, Thomas."

I turned to look down. "What's that? Where?"

"Steve Melton. He's not in here. He's been seen getting into a car not far from here—a white Toyota."

I stared down at her.

"You coming?" she asked.

I nodded then started to descend. I pushed the ladder back into the hitch and slammed it shut after me. I walked out of the walk-in closet, then paused, thinking I heard a noise.

"What are you doing?" Walsh said. "We need to move."

"I thought I heard something. A sound. It came from the attic."

"It's probably a rat."

"I don't like probably."

She threw out her hands. "Okay, then, it's definitely a rat."

I stared at the hitch in the ceiling of the closet. "Maybe I should go check it out after all? It'll only take a second. I don't like to leave any stones unturned."

"Argh, people are right when they say you're impossible. Okay, so let me ask you this. Did you hear any baby crying? I mean, we've been here in this house for quite some time now, and we haven't heard any baby crying. Babies cry. Or at least make noises. Lots of them."

I nodded, thinking of Angel, who always was so loud, especially when she woke up at night. She would often talk, blabber, or even sing what sounded almost like opera. Even as an infant, she made a lot of noise. Walsh was right.

"All right," I said and put my gun back in the holster. "You've made your point. We're leaving."

I glanced at the hitch one last time, then left the walk-in closet and shut the door behind me.

Chapter 31

WE DROVE BACK to the house where we met Rivers waiting for us outside. He looked frustrated.

"What have you got?" I asked as I approached him, jumping out of the car before Walsh had put it in park.

"Nothing. Dang it!" He rubbed the bridge of his nose.

"I thought you said that Melton was seen getting into a car?" Walsh asked.

She stood next to me, hands on her hips. She had those long legs that made her look amazing in pants. I always wanted that.

"Yes. One of my men talked to a neighbor who said that he saw Steve Melton running down the street, and then a white Toyota came up on his side, and he got in. All we know is that the Toyota went south and then took a right turn. The neighbor didn't know the car and had never seen it before. We've searched everywhere. We've combed through the entire neighborhood with no luck."

"And what about the baby?" I asked. "Did he have the baby with him when getting into the car?"

Rivers shrugged. "The neighbor couldn't see. He saw him

through the window, and there was a distance, plus he was hidden by the car. He could have been carrying something, but the neighbor couldn't say for certain if he was or not."

"But he was sure that it was Steve Melton?" I asked.

He nodded. "Yes. He's been living here for years and knows him very well. Says he is usually such a nice man and that he would never have thought he would hurt anyone, let alone a child."

"There are some things here that don't seem to add up," I said and looked at Walsh. "Have we showed a picture of Clarissa to any of the neighbors? If she lived with Steve Melton for fourteen years, people must have seen her around."

"Unless he kept her at another location," Walsh said. "One that no one here knows of."

I nodded. She made a good point.

"Let's find out if he has taken any leases on other houses or condos," I said. "Or if they have a summer cabin somewhere. Maybe even in his family's name; he could have inherited it or maybe bought it without the wife knowing. Check his credit card statements if nothing else works. Any regular payments could be rent or a mortgage. Chances are, if he kept Clarissa in another place, he will take baby Desiree there as well if she isn't there already. That would explain why the wife didn't know what we were talking about when asking about the baby."

"I'll take care of that," Walsh said, walking away with her phone clutched to her ear. "I've got the right guy who can find out quickly for me."

"I'll make sure my men ask about the girl," Rivers said. "Can you send me a recent picture of her?"

I did, and he left too. I stood behind, my stomach nervous and worried. I couldn't let go of the feeling that we could be looking for the wrong guy. Yet, it had to be him, right? It had to be Steve Melton. He was the one who got Clarissa pregnant. The DNA test showed it was. No, he was definitely our man. Yet I didn't feel any closer to finding the baby, and as the hours passed, so did the chances of her surviving. It was a race against time, and right now, we were the ones losing.

Big time.

Chapter 32

"THERE'S something you need to see."

Walsh came back and handed me her phone. I stared at the display and the article she wanted me to read. I skimmed through it.

"What the..."

I lifted my gaze and looked into her eyes, trying to calm my anger from erupting. This was the last drop for me.

"What is this?"

"It's in the *Post* today. It was published online this morning."

"But...but we barely knew his name this morning? How has Alexander Huxley found out and written this garbage before I even got here?"

Walsh shrugged. "He must have somehow gotten the results from the DNA test and the fact that we matched it with a name. Who knows?"

"And what is this?" I said and pointed. "He wrote that 'Sources within the police confirm that they believe Steve Melton is the man who kept Clarissa Smalls and has now taken baby Desiree.' Is he freaking kidding me? Sources within the police? Who are they?

Who is he talking to? Who is blabbering to him? What kind of an idiot would confirm this type of thing?"

"I don't know," Walsh said. "But I do know that most people believe it's you. You two go way back, and this has been happening a lot. No one believes it's on purpose, of course, but that he might sort of bait you into it from time to time."

I stared at her in disbelief. I went over my last meeting with him and every word I had said. I shook my head. Nope, I hadn't confirmed that part about Melton. There was no way I could have. I didn't know at the time. He had to have gotten it from somewhere else.

"I would...I would never tell this guy anything. Gosh, he annoys me," I groaned and handed her back the phone before I threw it against the pavement in anger. "Why would I tell him this and ruin the entire investigation? It makes no sense. Can't you see that?"

She nodded. "I see that, yes. But not all people think the way I do."

"I don't care what people think," I said and closed my jacket all the way up to make it cover my throat. I was getting cold out there and felt awful. There was no telling what kind of damage Alex could have done to our investigation by revealing that we had a suspect and even naming him. That was probably why he knew we were coming and took off.

"That little piece of...."

I shook my head in disbelief, then grabbed my phone, intending to call Alex and give him a piece of my mind. But then I remembered something and stopped myself.

"Wait a second," I said and looked at the house in front of us.

"What?" Walsh asked. "What are you thinking?"

"The name."

"What name?"

I looked at her while an idea was shaped in my head.

"A name is not just a name. Sometimes, it's more than that."

"What on earth are you talking about?" Walsh asked, sounding like she believed I had completely lost it now.

"Sometimes, a name has a meaning to a person or even an entire family."

She narrowed her eyes. "Still not getting it."

"You will," I said and started to walk up to the front door. "Just follow me."

Chapter 33

WE OPENED the door and hurried inside the house. The techs were still gathering evidence material in boxes and had stacked them in the foyer. I nodded at one of them, and he nodded back as I rushed toward the stairs. I took a few steps up and looked at the framed photographs they had hanging on the walls. I stared at one in particular, then down at Walsh, who was right next to me, one step below.

"What are we looking at?" she asked.

I pointed at the middle picture of the three. "They have a son."

"Yeah? So?"

I lifted my eyebrows, waiting for her to put together the pieces. She didn't, at least not fast enough, so I had to do it for her.

"Sometimes, people name their sons the same as themselves. You know to pass on the name."

"Steve Melton, Jr.?" she asked.

"Yes. We might have been looking for the wrong Steve."

"But the DNA...?"

"I asked Rivers, and he told me it wasn't a complete match. It was a close match. A partial match, he said. *It lit up in the system;*

LITTLE DID SHE KNOW

that's how it was expressed from the lab—enough to make them think he was the one. But this tells me we might actually be looking for someone related to him. As in maybe his son. Did they take in the mom yet?"

"I think she's still sitting in the patrol car outside," Walsh said.

"Excellent."

I hurried outside and found the patrol car with Dana Melton inside it. She was cuffed and sat with her head bent down when I asked an officer if I could have a quick word with her. He opened the door, and she looked up at me, her eyes red from crying.

"I told you I don't know anything about any baby," she said between sobs. "I haven't had a baby in the house for many years."

I knelt next to her then placed a hand on her shoulder. "I know. That's not what I want to ask you about."

She looked at me. "Then what?"

"Your son. We need to talk to him. Where do we find him?"

"Junior?" she said with a small shriek. "Why are you pulling him into this? Haven't I told you this is all a mistake?"

"I just need to talk to him. Where do I find him?" I asked.

"He's…either at his condo downtown or at work."

"He doesn't live here?"

"No. He moved out about eight months ago when he graduated high school. We wanted him to go to college, but he wanted to work instead, take time off to figure out what he wants to do with his life. He works at an Italian restaurant downtown as a bartender."

"Okay, we're gonna need the addresses for both places."

I took out my notepad and wrote it down as Dana told me both, then looked up at Walsh, who had been on the phone and was now putting it away.

"Got the name for the car," she said. "The white Toyota that Melton was seen getting into."

"Yes?"

"It's a rental. It was rented this morning at Dulles Airport under the name Linda Smalls."

I stared at her, thinking I had to have heard her wrong.

"Excuse me?"

"What? Does that name ring a bell?"

I ran a hand through my bangs while the information settled. "You could say that. What in the…what on earth is going on here?"

Chapter 34

"THANK you so much for giving me a lift."

Linda turned to look at the man sitting next to her in the car. She had rented it at the airport when she landed. She had taken the first flight out of town as soon as she read the article in the *Post*. A friend had sent it to her at six in the morning.

Have you seen this?

No, she hadn't. She didn't even know they had gotten the DNA results back for her daughter's baby. They knew who raped her, and they hadn't even told her mother.

The freaking bastards.

The police were useless. She couldn't trust any of them to do their job properly. She had waited for an hour, wondering what to do, then decided she needed to go there. Finding Steve Melton's address online wasn't hard; just one search, and she got it. She could even find his house on Google Maps and see what it looked like.

Then, she had decided to take matters into her own hands. The police didn't seem to be doing anything. So, she booked a flight for ten o'clock, then drove to the airport and took off. She had found the guy on Facebook and knew what the scumbag looked like.

She had been driving down his street when she saw him come running toward her on the sidewalk.

It's my lucky day.

"Do you need a ride?" she had asked, rolling down the window. She tried her best to sound sweet and like she was just trying to be nice.

Steve had smiled, relieved, then nodded.

"Yes, please. That would be amazing."

He did his best not to seem like a criminal on the run, and she did her very best not to seem like the revengeful mother she was in reality.

It went very well. Neither of them asked the other any questions, and they drove across town in silence.

Now, he was finally speaking to her. He seemed to have calmed down a little as he saw how easily they made it away from the neighborhood. He smiled at her. "You can just drop me off at the Amtrak Station. I can take a train from there."

"Oh, and where are you going?" she asked.

He looked out the window. "Just far away from here, I guess."

"Are you running away from something? Or someone?" she asked, trying to sound like she didn't already know why he was trying to get away.

"You could say that. I'd rather not talk about it," he said. "It's painful."

"I bet it is," she said as her hand caressed the gun she had stuck under her left thigh so he wouldn't see it. She hadn't thought it was possible, but she had actually managed to get it through airport security by tucking it into a box from an old hairdryer she had bought long ago and placing it in her checked suitcase. It had been a daring thing to do, but somehow, she had gotten away with it, much to her surprise.

"So, just drop me off over on the corner there," he said and pointed. "I can walk the rest of the way."

"I'm sure you can," she said and stepped on the accelerator as the light in front of them turned green. She rushed past the corner he had indicated, and Steve Melton complained.

"Hey, you missed it."

"I sure did," Linda said and looked at him, accelerating further, almost hitting a car door that was being opened from a parked car on the side of the road. Steve screamed and put his hands up as if he thought that would help protect him from the impact.

"Watch it. You're going way too fast. I need to get out of here."

She looked at him again, then pulled out the gun and cocked it, pointing it at him.

"I don't think so. I don't think you're going anywhere."

Chapter 35

STEVE MELTON, Jr. lived in a small, scrappy two-bedroom apartment in downtown DC, which he shared with a friend. He was home alone when we rang the doorbell. When he opened the door, he was in his bartender outfit, his hair still wet from showering.

I showed him my badge.

"FBI, can we have a chat?"

He looked nervously at me, then at Agent Walsh.

"S-sure. I have to get to work in half an hour, though."

"We'll make it quick," I said.

"O-okay," he said and stepped aside so we could walk in. Walsh went straight for the other rooms to look inside, searching for the baby, while I closed the door behind us and walked with him into the living room. He seemed anxious.

"What is this about?"

I showed him a picture of Clarissa.

"Do you know this girl?"

He shook his head after barely looking at it. "N-no. Never seen her before in my life."

"Nothing, no baby," Walsh said as she joined us in the living room.

Steve Melton, Jr. gave her a strange look. "Baby? What are you talking about… baby?"

I stared at him, scrutinizing him. Was this an act? He looked at Walsh, then down at me.

"Is that what this is about? Are you here because of the baby? I told her I didn't want it. I told her to get rid of it."

I smiled. "So, you do know Clarissa."

He shook his head. "No. That girl there, her name is Cate."

I lifted my eyebrows. "Oh, really? But you do know her?"

"I…we…had a thing. It didn't last long, okay? I know it was wrong. But I didn't know she was so young. I swear, I had no idea. She didn't tell me her age. I met her at the restaurant where she was hanging out in the bar with some friends. They had fake IDs. I assumed she was old enough. She didn't tell me her ID was fake until later—until after. We went back to my place, and we…well, you know."

"You got her pregnant."

"That was an accident. The last thing I wanted was a baby. Did she report me because of that? Because I told her I didn't want it?"

I stared at him, thinking this made a lot more sense. I couldn't quite fit the pieces together before since this Steve Melton would have been four years old when she was kidnapped. This guy hadn't kidnapped anyone; he had just screwed up by having sex with a minor and accidentally getting her pregnant.

"Where did Cate live?" I asked.

He shrugged. "I don't know. She never told me."

"What was her last name?"

He gave me a look, narrowing his eyes. "You don't know her name?"

"Just answer the question, please."

"I don't know."

"Let me get this straight. You slept with her and got her pregnant, but you don't even know her last name or where she lived? Did she talk about who she lived with? A father or a mother?"

He shook his head. "We didn't talk about that stuff. Listen, it was a one-night thing. That's all it was supposed to be. And I swear, I didn't know how young she was until she came here and told me she was pregnant. I freaked out, okay? I told her I never wanted to see her again. I told her to get rid of it."

"But you must have some sort of way to contact her. Did you have her phone number?"

He shook his head. "No, as I said, we only hooked up that one time, and then a few months later, she was standing by my door when I got home from work, and she told me she needed to talk to me. I let her inside, and she said she was pregnant. I freaked out completely. I'm not gonna be a dad."

"So, you threw her out and didn't even help her. That's nice," I said and signaled to Walsh that I had heard enough. "You're gonna do well in life."

Chapter 36

THEN:

"This guy has quite the rap sheet," Garcia said as they walked up to the small yellow house with the wrap-around porch. An old rusty car was parked in the driveway, and it didn't look like it had been driven anywhere in ages.

"What has he done?" Brent asked, walking up the steps to the porch.

"Burglaries. He's been in twice for house burglaries. Once for car theft."

Brent nodded. He was a scumbag—no doubt about it. That didn't mean he had taken a child.

"Okay, let's have a talk with him."

Brent opened the screen door and knocked. They waited for a few beats before knocking again.

Finally, the door opened. The guy in the doorway was big and tall. He was bald with a goatee. He had spilled something brown on his grey T-shirt.

"Yes?"

Brent showed him his badge. "Tom Wilder?"

"Who wants to know?"

"Detectives Brent and Garcia, may we come in?"

He looked flustered. "We can talk out here."

Tom Wilder closed the door behind him. Garcia sent Brent a concerned look. He knew what he was thinking, but there could be many reasons why he didn't want them inside. It didn't have to be because he had the baby in there. Besides, they'd hear her cry if she was in the house, right? Babies cried a lot.

Right?

Of course, they did. Everyone knew that.

"What is this about?" Tom asked with a sniffle.

Brent looked at Garcia to take over. They had agreed that he would take this one. It was good training for him. Garcia pulled out a picture of baby Anna. "We're searching for this child."

Tom glared at the picture. Then he wrinkled his forehead before shaking his head. "I haven't seen her."

Garcia scrutinized him. "You sure?"

He grimaced. "Of course, I'm sure. Why are you asking me?"

"You know the mother."

He threw out his hands. "I've known a lot of women."

"You knew her by her maiden name, Amelia Knox."

His smile froze.

"Right?" Garcia asked when he didn't say anything. "You used to date?"

"Yes, years ago."

Garcia nodded, biting the side of his cheek.

"That's awful," Tom Wilder added. "I did hear about a baby going missing on the news earlier, but I didn't know it was hers. I mean, how would I? I haven't seen her in years."

"Really? Because she told us you two met recently," Garcia said.

Tom Wilder looked at Garcia, then at Brent, then back at Garcia. "Oh, yeah, that's right. I met her by accident. I forgot about that."

Garcia paused.

"Really?" he asked. "You forgot?"

"Yes, I don't know what to tell you. I guess it didn't make a big impression because I had completely forgotten."

Garcia nodded. "I see. Can we take a look inside your house?"

Tom looked surprised, then nodded. "I don't see why, but knock yourselves out."

He opened the door and let them inside. Brent followed Garcia into the living room. They did a quick search around the two bedrooms and in the kitchen but found no trace of the baby.

"All right," Brent said. "Time to wrap it up. He obviously doesn't have her."

Garcia looked disappointed as they walked back to the car in the street. "I was just so sure."

Brent wrinkled his forehead. "Really? Why?"

"Didn't you notice how his hands shook and how his voice vibrated when talking to us? And he was sweating even though it was fifty-four degrees out, and he was just wearing a T-shirt. He was obviously very nervous."

That made Brent laugh as he unlocked the car. "He was also very cooperative. My guess is he probably did something else that he is scared we'd find out about. Probably another burglary. But he didn't take the baby."

"How can you be so certain?"

Brent tapped his nose.

"Instinct. One day, you'll have it too."

Chapter 37

"I THOUGHT IT WAS AN EASY OPERATION?"

I was in my motel room and had just sat down on the bed when Matt called. I had completely forgotten to keep him updated.

"You said you'd be back tomorrow?"

I exhaled and leaned back on the bed, placing my head on the pillow. I was so exhausted that I could have fallen asleep while still on the phone.

"That's what it was supposed to be, but it took an unexpected turn. You know how it is sometimes."

"He ran?"

"Yes, he got away, and then we realized he wasn't the one we were actually looking for. It was his son. He got the girl pregnant."

"But he didn't kidnap her? I don't understand," Matt said.

"Listen, I can't really tell you the details. You know this."

"I also know that we have a baby who misses her mother, and I have a life I want to go live. But now you're telling me you won't be back tomorrow after all?"

I sighed and pinched the bridge of my nose. "That's what I'm saying. The son wasn't the one who kidnapped her or took the baby, but he knows more than he's saying. I'm sure of it. I just don't know how to get it out of him. And don't get me started on his dad, who apparently knows Clarissa's mom."

"What? What are you saying?"

I closed my mouth. I had told him too much. Matt was a detective, so I was pretty sure he was safe to talk to, but I just had to be careful.

"I don't know," I said. "I'm so tired. I can't think straight."

"It sounds a little fishy, to be honest," Matt said. "The girl's mother knows the guy who kidnapped her daughter?"

"No," I groaned. "That's not what I said. I just...we need to find him. And baby Desiree. I'm certain she's here somewhere. We know that Clarissa lived here because this is where she got pregnant. We know she went by the name Cate but don't know the last name or where she was being kept."

"Sounds like you might be gone for a little more than one more day," Matt said with a deep groan.

I rubbed my eyes. "I...it's too early to say."

"But I should prepare myself to have Angel for longer," he said, annoyed. "Maybe even the rest of the week. That's great, Eva Rae. You really know how to ruin my life. And I can't really say no, can I? You leave me with no options. As usual. It's just so...typically you."

I sat up. This felt awfully familiar to what I had gone through in my marriage with Chad. I just really wished that Matt, of all people, would understand better since he was in the same line of work.

But apparently not.

"This is a matter of life and death," I said. 'This baby needs surgery. The clock is ticking. I can't just go home. I'm sorry if it's inconvenient for you, but what do you want me to do? I need to find this baby."

He went quiet for a few seconds. I could sense his anger

through the phone. "Just make sure you're back by Friday, okay? I have plans for the weekend, and I don't want to have to change them again."

"I'll try," I said.

"I'll see that before I believe it," Matt said and hung up without even saying goodbye. I hid my face between my hands and cried. How had I suddenly found myself in this same situation again?

Was it me?

Was I being unreasonable?

I didn't get to finish the thought before my phone vibrated again in my hand. It was Sheriff Dawson, and I picked it up immediately.

Chapter 38

"WHERE ARE YOU TAKING ME?"

Linda didn't even look at Steve Melton sitting next to her as she drove up the narrow road toward the house. She had found it on Airbnb while waiting for the airplane the day before and rented it.

It was a little pricey for a week in a four-bedroom house, but Linda didn't care. She needed something secluded and something fast.

"What is this place?" Steve asked and looked out the window. They had driven outside of DC and found the small place hidden away in a wooded area, located directly above a small lake. *A fisherman's paradise*, it was called in the ad.

But Linda wasn't going to be fishing.

Neither was Steve.

Linda stopped the car, and, still while pointing the gun at him, she told him to get out.

Still with his hands raised, he did as he was told, and they walked up to the front door. She punched in the code she had received in the app and opened the door.

"Get in."

He nodded and rushed inside. She locked the door behind them and kept the gun aimed at him. Then, she grabbed a chair, placed it in the middle of the living room, and asked him to sit on it. With duct tape she had bought at an ACE hardware store on her way to Steve's house, she tied him to the chair. He whimpered but didn't scream. She thought it was possibly because he knew it was futile. There were no neighbors nearby, and no one would hear it.

"W-why are you doing this?" he asked.

Linda took another dining chair and placed it in front of him, then she sat on it backward and put the gun on the back of it. She stared at him for a few seconds before answering.

"You took her."

"What?"

"You turned her against me. She doesn't know me at all, and she doesn't even want to know me."

"I...I don't...under...."

"My own daughter, the same girl I have dreamed of holding in my arms again for fourteen years, doesn't even want to talk to me. Do you have any idea what that is like?"

"N-no, but I can imag...."

She slammed the gun onto the top of the chair. Steve gasped.

"No, you can't! That's the thing. You really can't imagine what it is like if you haven't gone through it."

"O...okay, then, no, I can't imagine what it's like."

"She hates me. My own daughter hates me! And I didn't even do anything to her. You did. You did this to her...to me."

"Me? N...no. I didn't do...I ran from the police because I was scared. They have accused me of rape before, but I didn't do it. I was acquitted."

"Stop it." She yelled and got up. She kept the gun pointed at him. "I don't want to hear it. I don't want to hear your lies or excuses. You hurt me; you made my life a living hell. Do you know that I used to celebrate her birthday every year? And save a piece of cake in the fridge for her. Just in case she'd show up. Silly, right?"

He spoke between light gasps. "I…can't say…."

"Oh, I know it is. But that's the thing. When you're grieving like that, waiting, hoping, dreaming, you do lots of silly things. I would talk to her too, say good night to her every night before bed—wherever she was. Praying she was safe. But she wasn't. She wasn't safe. She was kidnapped, and kept, and raped…by you!"

Steve's eyes grew wide.

"Me? But…I have never…."

She placed the gun on his forehead, and he whimpered, his eyes closed.

"Shut up. Shut up with all your freaking lies. I don't care anymore. I have waited and waited and wanted this for so long. Barely making it through each day, struggling to keep myself going. Now, it's your time to suffer."

"But…I haven't done any…."

He had barely finished the sentence when Linda placed the gun on his knee and fired.

Chapter 39

"SHE'S GONE."

He was panting agitatedly into the phone as he spoke. It made him hard to understand.

"Who is? Linda? Because I think we...."

"No," Sheriff Dawson interrupted me. "Not Linda. Clarissa."

I shot up in the bed, suddenly wide awake.

"What?"

"Clarissa is missing. They called me tonight from the hospital. Apparently, she left there sometimes this afternoon. They've searched for her everywhere, at the hospital and in the surrounding area, but surveillance cameras captured her leaving through the back entrance, and then we believe she stole a car. Someone reported their gray Honda minivan stolen. We got the tags for the stolen car and have put out an alert, but so far have gotten nothing."

I stared at the wall in front of me inside my hotel room. There was a painting of a big willow tree in a field somewhere in a glass frame.

"H-how is this possible? I don't understand this at all. Didn't you have a guard by her door?"

"We don't know how she got past him. He said he was on his phone, and she might have snuck out, or maybe it happened when he was in the restroom or down for coffee. He doesn't know how long she was gone before he realized it, but the surveillance camera captured her by the back door at three o'clock, and the hospital didn't realize she was gone until five when a nurse entered her room to take some blood tests."

I closed my eyes. "Wow. That's bad. That's really bad. She could have been kidnapped again, for all we know."

Dawson went quiet at the other end. I could feel his embarrassment through the phone.

"Could the kidnapper have come back for her?" Dawson asked. "Would that be a behavior fitting with his profile?"

I bit my lip while a million thoughts rushed through my head. The kidnapper might be interested in silencing her. That would be his motive.

"But you said she was alone on the surveillance video, right?" I asked. "She left the hospital on her own."

"Yes."

I couldn't stop thinking about Steve Melton, Jr. Something wasn't right about him and what he had told us.

"I have a feeling she's coming here," I said.

"To DC?"

I nodded. "Yes. I have a feeling Steve Melton, Jr. hasn't told us everything he knows."

"I…I'm not sure I understand," Dawson said.

"It's okay," I said. "You don't have to."

I hung up, then dialed Walsh's number. "What's your go-to food for stakeouts?"

She laughed lightly. "Coffee."

"That's it? Coffee? We can never be friends."

"What's yours?" she asked.

"M&M's. Lots of them."

"Okay, I'll pick some up when I get my coffee on the way. I take it you want me to pick you up at the hotel?"

"You're thinking correctly. Make it two bags. It might be a long night."

"I rarely sleep anyway," she said.

"Me either. Maybe we can be friends after all."

"At least you'll have the M&Ms to yourself."

"Good point."

Part IV

48 hours later

Chapter 40

"SOMETHING IS TERRIBLY WRONG. I'm telling you. I need your help."

"Let me get this straight, sir. You're telling me your baby has been sleeping for more than twenty-four hours without waking up at all?"

"Yes, yes, that's what I'm saying. Please, help me."

He stared at baby Sandra. She was so small and fragile while lying on the bed. She was breathing very raggedly, and sometimes she would stop breathing completely for a longer time. It worried him. He had called a doctor, thinking they could help him over the phone.

"That sounds very serious, sir," the female doctor said. "I think you should bring her in as soon as possible."

"But I can't," he said, his voice shaking. "That is not an option."

"But sir..."

"Just tell me what is wrong with her, please. So I can fix it."

"I can't tell you over the phone, sir; I really think you should take her to the ER immediately."

"No! No! I can't do that."

"Well, I'm sorry, sir, but I will have to report this, then."

He gasped, then hung up. He stared at the phone in his hand. Would she report him? Could they then trace the call? He couldn't risk that. He shut off the phone but worried it wasn't enough. Then he split it open and took out the SIM card.

Was that enough?

He wasn't sure.

"Sandra, sweet baby Sandra, wake up for me, will you? Please?"

He rubbed her belly, hoping she would open her eyes, then tried to feed her the bottle when she didn't. The milk spilled on her lips, but she didn't eat—not even a drop of it.

It's been too long. She's sick!

"What do I do? What am I supposed to do?"

Panic erupted inside him, and he felt awful. He couldn't call anyone and let them know or ask for help. He was all alone in this.

Take her to the ER.

That's what the doctor had said. He knew she was right. At the ER, they'd know what to do. But how could he take her there? She might live, yes, but she would be taken away from him. He would go to jail. It was too risky.

What am I going to do?

Tears rolled down his cheeks as he stared at her tiny body on the bed. He shook his head while crying.

No, he had to do something. He couldn't just let her die. He had to save her somehow. And that was when he got an idea. He picked her up gently between his hands, then wrapped her in a blanket. He kept her close to his own body as he walked out of the house and put her in the car, then took off, passing the many police cars by the Meltons' house on his way, trying his best not to look so he wouldn't cause suspicion.

He nodded at a police officer walking toward his patrol car and smiled the best he could. The officer nodded back, and he continued on his way.

Just pretend like everything is normal.
Everything is normal.
Everything.

Chapter 41

I TURNED the bag of M&M's upside down and poured out the last one into my hand. I stared at it for a little with a deep sigh, then ate it and dropped the empty bag to the floor of the car, where it landed next to the other three bags I had devoured these past two days.

I looked at the building in front of us. All the lights were shut off in the windows. It was three in the morning, and I struggled to stay awake. Next to me, in the driver's seat, Walsh was sleeping and snoring lightly. We were taking turns to sleep a few hours. She had pushed her seat down, but I could still see that she was uncomfortable. Now, she blinked and opened her eyes.

She raised her seat and sat up straight. "Anything?"

I shook my head then showed her the empty candy bag.

"That bad, huh?"

I exhaled and leaned back in my seat. My back was starting to ache from sitting in the same position for hours. I needed to stretch my legs.

"So, how long do you think we will have to keep an eye on him?" Walsh asked. "It's been two days. All he has done is go to work, go to the store and buy groceries, then go home and sleep. What if the girl isn't coming here after all?"

"It takes twelve hours to drive here," I said and looked at my watch.

"She would be here by now," Walsh said. "Even if she made a few stops on the way. It's been two freaking days."

I nodded. She was right. I just really didn't want to give up yet. I was so sure Steve Melton, Jr. was hiding something.

"I'm really tired," Walsh said and yawned. She picked up her cup and shook it. "And we're out of coffee."

"All right," I said, feeling the tiredness nag at me. "She's not coming. Let's go home and get some re…."

I paused when seeing something. Walsh was in the middle of stretching when she noticed too.

"Is that…?"

"Yup," I said and felt suddenly wide awake. "That's Steve, and it looks like he's leaving."

"In the middle of the night?" Walsh said.

I nodded. "This could be something."

Walsh cleared her throat and looked at me. "Could also be a booty call."

I nodded, then opened the car door and stepped out.

"I'm taking the chance."

I closed the door as quietly as possible, then closed my coat and hurried after him, keeping a beat behind him so he wouldn't see me. He turned a corner, and I ran a few steps to make sure I didn't lose him. At the end of the block, he suddenly stopped, and so did I, hiding in the entrance of an apartment building.

It took a few minutes before a car drove up next to him and stopped. He opened the door on the passenger side and jumped in. I took pictures with my phone as they drove past me, and I got a quick glimpse of the driver.

Walsh drove up on my side, and I jumped in. We followed their car through town. It was snowing now and hard to see ahead of us.

"Was it her?" Walsh asked. "Was it the girl?"

I shook my head. "No. It was a man. And I have a feeling I've seen him somewhere before. I just can't figure out where."

Chapter 42

THEN:

Ron and Amelia were in the kitchen when they got back. Ron jumped to his feet, sweat springing to his forehead.

"Where is she? Did you find her?"

His voice was shivering heavily, and his eyes stared almost manically at Agent Brent. Garcia shook his head.

"I'm sorry. She wasn't there."

"But...How...?"

Ron grunted angrily, then placed both his hands on his head.

Quite the actor.

"Are you sure you looked everywhere? Did you take him into the station? Did you interrogate him?"

Brent stepped forward, placing his fingers in his belt, puffing himself up. "Are you asking me if I did my job properly?"

Ron groaned loudly and wasn't even trying to hide his frustration. He was beyond that point now.

"Oh, God, please tell me you're at least keeping an eye on this guy. Please, say that you have a patrol car out there following his every move, right?"

"Don't tell me how to do my job," Brent said, pointing his finger at him. He was getting pretty tired of this guy by now. "I'm telling you we searched his place thoroughly and found no trace of your child. Why are you so interested in making this guy look guilty?"

They stared into each other's eyes, and Brent saw the guilt written in Ron's. There was no doubt in his mind. He was just trying to get their attention away from himself. It was so obvious and so typical.

Ron threw out both arms. "Did you at least check to see if he could be hiding her somewhere else? Might he have a cabin somewhere? An apartment? Maybe he's keeping her at a friend's place?"

Ron stared from one to the other. His face was turning red, and the vein on his throat was popping out. *This guy is about to have a heart attack,* Brent thought. *Guilt can do that to you. It can drive you nuts and make you sick.*

"Hello?" Ron asked. "Did you at least check everything out? His background?"

"We did," Garcia said confidently. "He's got a long rap sheet."

"Isn't that evidence enough?" Ron asked. "He's a criminal. I'm sure he has our daughter. Why don't you take him in? Why don't you arrest him?"

"Let's not get ahead of ourselves here," Brent said and raised a hand to try and calm Ron down. "We have no reason to believe this man has taken your child. We checked him out and ran his background, and yes, he has a couple of burglaries on his conscience and a car theft too, but there were absolutely no indications that he has kidnapped your child. There really isn't much more we can do at this point. He's not our guy."

"Because you didn't try hard enough," Ron said, taking a step forward. "Look at us. Look at my wife. We're completely broken here, and what are you two doing about it? What are you doing to find our kid? Absolutely nothing. You're letting the one guy go who could actually have done it. And instead, you're here? Why? You should be out there looking for our child, for crying out loud."

Ron took another step forward, lifting his arm in the air aggressively.

"Sir, I need you to step back," Garcia said.

But he didn't listen. Instead, Ron stepped forward, grabbed Brent by the shoulders, and started to shake him.

"Please. Can't you just find our baby? Please?"

"That's it."

Brent grabbed him by the wrist, then yanked his arm back until Ron fell to his knees. Then he placed handcuffs on his wrists and closed them.

"What are you doing?" Amelia screamed while Garcia read Ron his Miranda rights.

"We're taking him in," Brent said with a snort. "We're arresting him."

Chapter 43

THE STREETS WERE EERILY EMPTY. Not that it was strange at this time of night, but still. Washington, DC always had some sort of activity. At least that's how I remembered it. But not this night. Maybe it was the snow that was keeping people indoors. We didn't meet a single car as we drove across town, following Steve Melton, Jr. closely, yet not so close he might see us. It was easier said than done. There was no way of blending in on this freezing cold night.

"There. He's stopping by that building over there," I said and pointed. "Just keep going."

Walsh did as I said, and we drove slowly past them, seeing Steve get out of the passenger side. We continued on, then parked at the end of the street where they couldn't see us anymore. Then I got out and rushed back, running cautiously since the snow made the sidewalk slippery.

I put on the hoodie of my coat and held it closed to cover my throat and chin from the freezing wind.

I suddenly remembered very well what it was like living up here and became grateful for the warm Florida weather. I didn't miss this; that was for sure. I missed a lot of other stuff, but certainly not this.

The snow became denser, and it was harder for me to see. But I did spot Steve and the man just as they entered the building where they had stopped. I hurried but didn't make it to the door before it was slammed shut. I stared at the names on the display. Seven apartments, seven names.

"Did you see which one they pressed?"

Walsh had come up behind me. She, too, was covering herself the best she could with a hoodie. She had also found a scarf to wrap around her neck, which was smart. I was already freezing terribly.

I shook my head.

"Nope. It could be any of these."

She looked at the names, then shrugged. "Should we get back to the car and wait for them to come back out? We can run the license plate while we wait."

I nodded. Using my phone, I took a picture of the building, the house number, and the names on the intercom, then put my hands back in my pockets along with the phone. We ran through the snow back to the car and got in. Walsh started it back up, and we turned on the heat on high, then placed our hands on the blowers to warm them. Slowly, I got the sensation back in my fingers.

"What do you think he's doing?" Walsh asked and looked at the building down the street from where we had parked.

I shrugged. "Beats me."

I looked through the photos on my phone. I had gotten a very blurry one of the car's driver, but it was hard to see him properly.

"If only I knew where I have seen him before. It's really annoying," I grunted.

"Let me see."

I showed it to her. She squinted and zoomed in the picture, then shook her head. "It's really hard to tell."

"I got one of the license plate, too. Let's run it, along with the names of whoever lives in this building. Maybe that'll give us some answers because I'm running out of theories here."

Walsh grabbed her phone. "I'll do it right away."

Chapter 44

"OH, my God. Oh, my God! You…you shot me!"

Steve was talking through the pain while staring down at his knee. Blood was gushing onto the floor below. Linda stared at it, a little surprised at how much it was and how loud the man had screamed when she fired the gun at his knee. Linda had never fired a gun before and still had a ringing in her ears from the loud noise.

Now, what?

Shooting him didn't feel as satisfying to Linda as she had thought it would. Hurting him was all she had been able to think about since she heard that they knew who had taken Clarissa and kept her for fourteen years. She didn't want to kill him. At least not at first. She wanted to hurt him, make him suffer for all he had done to Clarissa.

Kidnapping her.

Raping her.

The very thought brought a new wave of anger up in Linda, and she lifted her nose toward the ceiling, then looked down at the screaming man.

"Stop whining," she said.

He lifted his gaze and looked at her through bloodshot eyes. His mouth was strained in a scream, but no sound left his lips anymore.

"You've just been shot in the leg," she continued. "It's nothing compared to what else I will do to you."

"I...what did I ever do to you?"

She felt the heavy gun in her hand, then walked closer and placed it against his shoulder. Steve squirmed in his seat.

"No, not again, please. I'm sorry for whatever it is you believe I have done. I'm sorry. I'm so, so sorry."

Linda tilted her head as she stared down at the worm of a man beneath her. He really was pathetic. She thought about Clarissa, and pictures of him on top of her, raping her, entered her mind as they had so many times before. But this time, they felt overwhelming—like she couldn't bear them; she couldn't bear the weight of them anymore. It was just too painful.

"You...took her," she said through tears.

"Took who?" he asked.

She growled and stared down at him. "You know very well who!"

He shook his head, tears of despair rolling from his eyes. "No. No, I don't! I really don't know."

Linda closed her eyes briefly, trying to push back the anger that was flooding her. She could almost not contain it. It was too much for her. The bastard refused to admit what he had done.

Rape. That's what the sheriff called it.

Him on top of her.

Panting.

Clarissa screaming, crying, begging for his mercy.

Linda opened her eyes. There was no mercy in hers, just like there hadn't been in his when taking what he thought was his, what he thought himself entitled to.

"I'm in pain," he whimpered. "Please, help me."

Linda took a deep breath then placed the gun on his shoulder again. "You don't know what pain is. Not yet."

Chapter 45

STEVE MELTON, Jr. came out of the building, followed by the other man. We could see them from afar and watched them get into the car and drive away. Then Walsh followed them back to the condominium where Steve lived, where he was dropped off. The vehicle then took off, and we stayed by Steve's condo.

"It's your turn to sleep," Walsh said, addressed to me. "We still have a few hours till sunrise."

I nodded, thinking it would be a smart move to get some rest. I was beyond exhausted, but even when I pushed my seat back and closed my eyes, I simply couldn't fall asleep. My head was spinning like crazy, and I kept wondering where I had seen the man before.

Finally, I dozed off, and when I woke up, the sun had risen, and it was bright out.

"Morning," Walsh said, sounding as tired as I felt.

I looked at her, and she continued.

"He's still up there."

"Okay."

I yawned and looked at my phone, then took it out of the charger. I had received a text. It was from Alexander Huxley.

I HEAR YOU WENT FOR THE WRONG GUY? CARE TO COMMENT?

"How the heck does he know that?" I mumbled.

"How does who know what?" Walsh asked.

I shook my head and put my phone in my pocket.

"Nothing. It's not important."

Yet, I couldn't stop thinking about it. If Alex wrote this in his paper, we would look like fools.

My phone vibrated, and I looked at it.

It was him again.

THE GIRL IS GONE?"

"Shoot."

I rubbed my forehead. I knew that they were trying to keep Clarissa's disappearance a secret, but, of course, it was just a matter of time before the media heard about it. I had told Dawson that and encouraged him to do a press conference instead, involving the press and the public in the search to avoid it becoming a scandal, but he wouldn't listen. He believed he would find her before the press heard about her disappearance.

"She can't make it far," was his argument. "She's a fourteen-year-old girl for crying out loud."

I had thought he didn't know much about teenage girls but didn't say anything.

"Now, what?" Walsh asked.

I looked up at her.

"Nothing, I just need to answer this."

Another text rolled in:

CAN YOU CONFIRM THIS?

I felt sick to my stomach. Of course, I couldn't.

"You might wanna do it fast," Walsh said. "Whatever it is."

I looked up from my screen.

"Why?"

"Because a gray Honda Minivan with Florida tags just pulled up."

Chapter 46

THEN:

"You can't do this to me."

Brent and Garcia sat down in the chairs across from Ron in the interrogation room.

"I didn't do anything."

"Let's just all calm down a little, okay?" Brent said.

"Calm down? Calm down? How am I supposed to calm down when my baby is missing, and you're doing absolutely nothing to find her?"

Brent sighed and tapped his fingers on the table, wondering how he would break this guy. He was a tough nut, for sure. They had gotten nowhere with him so far.

"We need you to go over…."

"Not again! Not again!" Ron interrupted him, yelling. "No. No. NO!"

Garcia leaned forward, folding his hands on the table. "You need to answer our questions."

"No, I don't. Because I already did. You want me to tell you my whereabouts the night before my daughter disappeared, what I did, and who I was with. Then you want me to tell you where I was that night when I've told you—so many times—that I was sleeping. Why didn't I hear anything? You will ask. How was it that a kidnapper could have known that the back door was left unlocked on this particular night when it is usually always locked? And am I sure that it was Amelia who forgot to lock it? All those stupid, stupid questions that I have already answered. So. Many. Times. You're driving me crazy."

"We still need all the facts," Garcia said, trying to sound calm. Brent could hear he was struggling with it now. "If we go over them again and again, it's to make sure we don't make any mistakes. And because there might be something we haven't seen or heard, something important we might have missed."

Ron leaned back in his chair. "I just…I can't take it anymore. I want to talk to my lawyer."

"And he is on his way," Brent said.

"I'm not saying anything else until he gets here," Ron said. "I just…I can't…. You're not listening anyway. Meanwhile, my baby… she's out there in the hands of some sick bastard. I swear…if she turns up dead, I will…."

"Just tell us what you did with her, you bastard," Brent said, standing to his feet. He had lost his patience with this idiot. "Here's what I think," he continued. "You got annoyed with her. She was crying at night, am I right? Constantly, incessantly crying and crying and wouldn't stop. So, you shook her to make her stop. Desperately, you shook her, and that was it, right? She became quiet because you shook her too hard. You killed her. It wasn't on purpose; it was an accident. You couldn't help it. What did you do to her after? Did you bury her in the yard? Because we will find her if you did. The dogs will sniff her out. Or maybe you took her somewhere and dumped her like garbage? In a dumpster, perhaps? Or a lake?"

Ron stared at Brent, eyes wide.

"H-how can you…NO!"

A light knock on the door interrupted them, and a woman poked her head in. Garcia went to chat with her, then came back.

"Your lawyer is here."

Garcia and Brent gathered their files, and Brent sent Ron a look as he walked out and made room for the lawyer to see his client. He was pretty sure that he saw a smile spread on Ron's lips as their eyes met.

Chapter 47

IT WAS HER. I was holding my breath as I stared at the gray Honda, and the door opened. Someone stepped out, and I recognized her immediately.

"You were right," Walsh said. "I can't believe it."

"I had a feeling that she and Steve Melton, Jr. were more than a one-night stand," I said.

"I think you might be right. What do we do next? You wanna take her in?" Walsh placed a hand on the door handle, but I stopped her.

"Not yet. Let her go to him."

Walsh let go of the handle and leaned back, then gave me a look. "Shouldn't we be getting the girl back to her mother in Florida?"

"Those two are holding the key to finding baby Desiree," I explained. "That's my theory. And that is more urgent right now."

We watched as she rang the bell and then waited. She spoke, and then the door was buzzed open. Clarissa looked to the sides like she was making sure no one saw her go in, then pushed the door open and went inside.

I could feel Walsh's eyes on me.

"Now, what?"

It was a valid question. But I didn't have an answer. I had some idea of what I wanted to do, but I wasn't sure it would work. It all depended on those two and what they did next. It was risky because we could end up losing sight of Clarissa, but it was worth it if she could somehow take us to the kidnapper.

"You think she's gonna go see her kidnapper next, don't you?" Walsh asked. "How can you be so certain?"

I shrugged. "I'm not, but I have a feeling that there's a reason she protected him and wouldn't tell us where she's been. At first, I believed she was in love with him. But now, I believe it's something else."

Walsh nodded. "Stockholm syndrome?"

"Something like that," I said as the door opened to the building again, and I spotted Clarissa and Steve walking out together. Clarissa had put on a beanie, and I guessed that Steve had given it to her so she wouldn't freeze.

He cared more about her than he had led us to believe. I had seen it in his eyes when he spoke about her. There was something there, a spark that told me he didn't mean it, that he was sad she was gone.

He put his arm around her shoulder as they walked down the street. I got out of the car and walked to the pavement, then followed them as closely as possible. When they reached the window of a store, they stopped and kissed. Steve was holding her head between his hands, and she was on her tippy toes to better reach him. It looked almost like a picture in a magazine with snowflakes dancing around them or some romantic movie scene.

I stopped too and hid behind a corner while they kissed. I was freezing, and I hugged myself to try and keep warm. Then I thought about Alexander Huxley. I don't know why since he was the last person I wanted to see. But for just a second, I thought about what it would be like to kiss him the way those two were kissing right now. It was so strange the way I felt about him. I remember being attracted to him back when I first met him, but also that I found him extremely annoying. He was too full of himself. But back then, I was married. I couldn't really allow myself to fall for him or even feel attraction. But that had changed. I was single now, and I still found him attractive.

But he could never know that. He would be impossible to be around. It would go to his head.

They began to move forward again, and I decided I was an idiot for even thinking like that. Alex was a pompous prick, and if he knew how I felt about him, I would not hear the end of it.

It was an absolute no-go.

Chapter 48

HE WAS BITING his nails excessively, as he always did when feeling anxious. His mom would always yell at him when he did it as a child, and now he could hear her voice in his mind.

Stop doing that.

But even though he knew he ought to stop, he couldn't. Not while waiting for news about baby Sandra. He was sitting in the foyer when the door opened, and the guy came out.

He sprang to his feet. "How is she?"

The doctor looked at him from behind his glasses. Then he shook his head. "I have to say; it doesn't look good."

"What do you mean? You...you can help her, right?"

The doctor shook his head. "I've done everything I can for her, but she needs to go to the hospital. I think she needs surgery. My guess is it's a heart defect, and she has had it since birth."

He shook his head. "Surgery. No, no. That's not an option. Isn't there some medicine she can take? Can't you do it?"

The doctor sent him a strange look. "I really can't. I'm just a pediatrician, and I took her in as a favor since I understood this was urgent and had to be done with discretion. But this is more than I can handle, I'm afraid. Her heart isn't beating as it should. I'm sorry, but you have to take her to the hospital. I can call for an ambulance."

The doctor handed Sandra to him. She was so tiny that it almost hurt to look at her.

He nodded. "There's no need. I'll handle it. I got her from here. Thank you, Doctor."

"Are you sure? It's no bother. She's very sick and needs immediate medical attention. I really think you should...."

He lifted his hand to stop him from talking. He was getting very annoyed with this guy right now.

"It's okay. I'll take care of it."

He left with Sandra, holding her close to his chest, got her in the car seat, and drove off. Then, he made a call.

"Yes, the doctor said she needs surgery. It's her heart."

He was almost crying when he said the words.

"What do I do?"

He went silent while the person on the other end gave him instructions. Then, he nodded.

"Okay."

He hung up, then looked at the baby with a deep sigh. He reached inside the car seat and caressed her cheek gently.

"Hold on, little baby Sandra," he whispered. "Just for a little while longer, then everything will be okay. I promise you; it will. Please, just hold on, okay? Don't die on me now. I know we can get through this together. Daddy has got a plan, okay? Daddy has got a plan, and I'm certain it will work. Just hang on, sweetie. Hang on for daddy. You can't give up now."

Chapter 49

THEY WERE GOING out for breakfast. Of course, they were. They had just been reunited after a long time apart, and she had been driving for days, maybe even all night. Naturally, they were starving.

I walked into the restaurant and sat at the bar, ordering some eggs and coffee for myself while keeping an eye on them. The coffee felt like it was heaven-sent after a long night in the car with Walsh.

Walsh had wanted to take them in for questioning—grill them until they finally told the truth and gave them names. But I had told her that wasn't my style. They had refused to talk to us until now; why would that have changed? They had no reason to want to speak to us now.

I still believed my plan was better, even though I wasn't sure it would work. They seemed so into one another that I began to wonder if they'd even go see the kidnapper.

What if Clarissa had actually only come here...*wait a minute.*

I paused and stared at them together, then realized something. Clarissa was fourteen years old. How did she know how to drive a car? She couldn't get a learner's permit until she was almost sixteen in Washington, DC. Driving from Florida to Washington wasn't a small task, especially if you hadn't driven a car before. I took out my phone and Googled it. There were ten states where you could start driving at fourteen. Had I misunderstood something?

It made no sense.

The two of them paid and got up, then walked out. I did the same and followed them back to Steve's apartment building. I found Walsh in the car, jumped in, then rubbed my fingers against one another and blew on them.

"Turn up the heat, please. I'm freezing."

"I got the names and backgrounds of who lived in the building where we saw Steve go last night. I wrote them down for you."

She handed me a piece of paper, and I looked at the names.

"Anything you can use?"

I shook my head. "Just looks like a lot of normal people. They could be friends. But why did they go there in the middle of the night?"

Walsh shrugged. "Beats me."

"I can't see why they'd visit any of these people. Most of them are retired...like this guy, who is a retired pediatrician from...."

I looked up at her. She turned her head and stared at me.

"What?"

"It might be a long shot, but what if...."

"I'm not following."

"The man. The one that picked up Steve last night. He was older than him, a lot older. It wasn't a friend."

"Then who do you think it was?"

I shook my head. "I can't let go of the thought that...the baby needs a doctor. What if..."

Walsh stared at me. "What if Steve helped him last night and took him to see a pediatrician? A retired one, someone he knew well who would do him a favor and wouldn't report it."

"Exactly. It's far-fetched; I know that, but still. I mean, I don't even know how they know one another."

Walsh threw out her hands.

"But if it is true, then the baby was right in front of us last night, and we missed it."

My heart dropped as the realization sank in.

"We missed it."

I paused. "But we have the license plate, right? Did we ever get the name of who owns the car?"

Walsh nodded. "It was a company car. Registered to Telp Industries. It's a big company with more than six thousand workers."

Chapter 50

HER FINGER MOVED on the trigger. Steve closed his eyes with a whimper as Linda pressed the gun against his shoulder. She wanted desperately to hurt him. She wanted him to beg for her mercy, to scream in pain. Just like she imagined Clarissa had day after day, year after year, while he kept her locked up.

Hurting her.

Raping her.

Steve screamed as she moved her finger, and then she screamed too—in anger, frustration, madness. She got herself ready to pull the trigger, and as the screaming stopped, when she was running out of air, she was panting and agitated, looking down at him below her. Then, she stopped. There was something that made her look up.

A sound. A noise.

A freaking knock on the door?

"What the...?" she asked and removed the gun from his shoulder. Steve whimpered as she stared at the front door behind her.

Another knock followed. And then, "Hello? Anyone home?"

Steve looked up at her, desperation in his eyes. He opened his mouth and yelled at the top of his lungs.

"HEL…"

Linda was on top of him. She placed a hand over his mouth and the gun against his cheek.

"Say one word, and I will kill you," she whispered in his ear.

"Hello? Anyone home?" the voice said from outside the door again.

Linda groaned. This person could have heard them. She would have to try and get rid of them.

"One second, please."

She yelled it, then stared down at Steve, shaking her head. "Not a single word or I swear I will shoot you in the head. Your face will look like that knee."

He whimpered, and she moved away from him cautiously. She was walking backward while keeping an eye on him. She didn't trust him for a second.

"Hello?"

"Coming right out," she said, then signaled for Steve to keep his mouth shut by placing the gun on her lips. Then she walked to the door and cracked it open, so only her face would be shown while she was holding the gun in her hand behind it, ready just in case.

Linda smiled.

"Yes?"

The man standing outside looked a little confused. He was older, maybe in his sixties, and had lost most of his hair but compensated for it by growing a big beard and wearing a baseball cap. He was a big guy, and she wouldn't be able to take him if it came down to a fight.

Luckily, she had her gun right behind the door.

"How can I help you?"

"I think I'm lost," he said with a concerned look. "Say, are you okay, ma'am? I stopped to ask for directions, but then as I stepped out of my truck, I heard someone scream."

Linda swallowed to make sure her voice didn't sound like she was in distress. She needed to calm her beating heart. She had genuinely believed that no one would hear them scream out here so far away from civilization, but apparently, she had overestimated that.

She smiled again, softly. "Yes, I am just fine."

"But…the screaming. It sounded serious?" he asked.

"Oh, that. It's nothing—it was just the TV. My husband loves to watch horror movies. I have never been into them, but what can you do, right?"

The man eased up slightly, and his shoulders came down. "Oh. I see. My wife loves those romantic chick flicks, and I hate them but don't tell her that. I watch them anyway, just for her sake."

"So, you know what it's like," Linda said with an uncomfortable chuckle. "What people won't do to keep their marriage going, right?"

"Right," he said. "I guess I'll just leave you…Say, you wouldn't know where the Sorensons live, would you? They told me number 235, but I went to that address, and the house looked abandoned. Maybe they gave me the wrong house number? They should be around here somewhere."

Linda shook her head. "I really don't. We're just renting this place for a few days. Airbnb, you know?"

"Ah, that makes sense. Okay. I won't take up more of your time. I'll leave you to your movie then." He lifted his cap slightly. "Have a good one."

"You too," Linda said, smiling widely.

"HELP. I'M IN HERE!"

Linda's heart dropped. It was Steve yelling from behind her. The man stopped on the steps and looked up at her, and Linda laughed awkwardly. The man stared at her, his brown eyes worried. Then, he eased up again.

"Maybe you should ask your husband to turn down the sound a bit, huh?"

"I keep saying that to him, but do you think he'll listen to me?"

"Sounds like he needs hearing aids," the man said, "That might help."

"I'll try and talk to him about it," Linda said with another smile while watching the man go to his pick-up truck, wave at her, then get in and take off. She waited until he was out of sight down the road, then slammed the door shut with a grunt.

"What the hell was that?" she yelled and ran toward Steve in the chair. Fear sprang to his eyes as she placed the gun on his cheek again.

"I told you I would freaking kill you if you said anything."

Then, she paused and eased up.

"Oh, you want me to kill you, don't you? You want me to get it over quickly, so you don't have to suffer the way I want you to because of what you did. But you're not getting off that easily, my friend. I have plans for you, big plans, and they're not to kill you yet."

She removed the gun from his face, and he stared at her, nostrils flaring, eyes wide and scared.

Then, she placed the gun on his tied-down hand in the back and pulled the trigger.

Chapter 51

"THIS IS the baby I'm talking about."

I showed Dr. Green the picture on my phone of baby Desiree that her mother, Sierra, had sent me. It was taken just after she was born. The retired Dr. Green looked at it through his glasses, then shook his head. We were sitting in his living room, in a beautiful old condo with stucco moldings and a wrought-iron staircase leading to a loft upstairs.

"I'm afraid I don't know what you're talking about. I haven't seen any baby," he said.

I glared at him, scrutinizing him closely. It made him uncomfortable, and he tapped his fingers on his knees. He was biting the inside of his cheek. That was his tell, I guessed.

"Do you live here alone?"

He nodded. "I was divorced seven years ago."

No biting; he was telling the truth. I saw something in his eyes —like a shadow rushing over them. He was feeling guilty.

"You do know that the baby is very, very ill, right?" I asked.

That made him freeze. His lips weren't moving, and he was barely breathing for a few seconds.

"I know you saw the baby because she is sick. I'm sure you told them to take her to the hospital, am I right?"

He stared at me. His eyes looked frightened.

"He didn't do it, did he?" he asked. "He didn't take her to the hospital so she could have surgery?"

"Nope," I said.

Dr. Green clasped his mouth and rubbed his face. "I knew it. I should have called for that ambulance or called nine-one-one. I just…I didn't know how to explain all this."

"You were scared you'd get in trouble?"

"Well, of course. I examined the baby and monitored her for the night; then, he came to pick her up. It was a favor. I've known Steve Melton, Jr. since he was born. I was stationed in Afghanistan with his father, Steve Melton, Sr. I didn't like it, but I thought, what can go wrong? I'm just helping someone out, someone who is sick. It's what I love to do; it's what I have done all of my adult life." He turned to face me, then placed a hand on my arm. "Please, tell me the baby hasn't died. She was in bad shape when they brought her to me. I have been so worried."

"Who brought her in?" I asked. "Who was the guy?"

He shook his head. "I don't know. I was told it had to be done discreetly. I believe in helping people, no matter what. In this case, I couldn't, though. There was nothing I could do."

"Did he give you a name?"

"No."

"Would you be able to describe the man who brought in the baby?"

He nodded. "Of course. He was taller than me, maybe six feet two, or about that. He was about two hundred pounds, I'd say. He had blond hair, was about twenty years younger than me, probably, so somewhere in his fifties."

I wrote it all down, then looked up at him again. "We'll need to get a drawing made. Can you help us with that?"

"Of course. I feel terrible. I want to help," Dr. Green said. Then he got up, walked to a dresser, and pulled out an envelope. He handed it to me. "He gave me this for my help. But I don't want it. There's five thousand dollars in there. I don't want that money. I feel so awful."

I took the envelope of money to put in as evidence. I got up and was about to leave when he grabbed my hand. "Please, find the baby before it's too late. Her heart. I'm not sure she'll make it through until tomorrow."

Chapter 52

THEN:

"Would any of you mind telling me what the heck is going on in your case?"

Garcia looked at his fingers, then up at Brent. He was nervous. They had been called into the captain's office after the lawyer had talked to her. The captain tapped her fingers on the desk.

"Come on, guys. I'm swamped with cases these days. I put you two on this one because Brent is so experienced, and I figured that you, Garcia, would learn something. I believed with you two, I was safe, and we could get the case solved without problems. But then I get a lawyer in my office complaining about you two? Saying that you're focusing on his client without grounds and not on finding his child?"

She stared at both of them, then threw out her hands.

"Who wants to begin? What's going on here? And please don't trip over one another to be first."

Brent leaned back in his chair and placed his hands behind his head. He refused to be intimidated by some young captain—and a woman on top of it. He knew perfectly well why they had made her captain so young—because of her freaking sex. They wanted more females in leading positions within the force, so as long as you showed up with a pair of tits, you were almost certain to be someone's boss within a year or two. It was just the way things were these days. Not like in the old days, when you had to earn it.

"Brent?" she asked, folding her hands on the desk between the many stacks of case files. She looked tired and a lot older than when she had come to the station six months ago. And she had gained weight. She was very skinny when she first got there, but now she was getting a little chubby around the hips and the chin. It was too bad. He had thought she was very pretty when he first saw her. Now, she was just letting herself go. It was really sad.

"Listen," he said. "We're focusing on the dad because I'm certain he is hiding something."

The captain bit her lip and looked at him. "What do you have to support that suspicion?"

Brent pointed at his nose. "This."

She tilted her head. "A hunch. You know that's not enough. You arrested the guy. Why?"

"He attacked me," Brent said. "Garcia is my witness."

Garcia nodded.

"It's true."

The captain closed her eyes briefly. She didn't look well, and Brent worried she would be sick. She leaned forward with a slight groan and touched the side of her abdomen.

"Are you okay, ma'am?" Garcia asked and stood to his feet.

She nodded. "Just a little stomach issue. It'll pass. Our child brought home some bug from daycare. I'll be fine."

"Maybe you should go home," Brent said. "Get some rest."

She waved to make him stop fussing. Brent sat back down.

"Do we have any other suspects?" she asked.

Garcia nodded. "There was an ex-boyfriend that we talked to, and I found him suspicious."

Brent scoffed. "He's a small-time criminal, you know—car thefts and so on. Hardly a baby snatcher or even a killer. I know the dad did it; I just need to put a little more pressure on him, then he will confess. I've seen cases like this many times before. There was nothing that told us the ex-boyfriend had anything to do with it."

She exhaled and looked at them. "Listen, guys. I trust you. If you think the dad did it, focus on him, and leave the ex-boyfriend alone. Find me that baby, or at least find out what happened to her. I have the press breathing down my neck, and I have all these cases to review. This is a high-profile case, especially since the mom is one of our own. I just want it off my desk as fast as possible. If you say the guy is a suspect, then I believe you. But get solid evidence, and get it fast. The clock is ticking, and the public is asking for answers. I'll take care of the lawyer. We can keep the dad here until tomorrow, but no longer. Find me that baby. Now. And get out of my office before you get whatever it is I have."

Chapter 53

I CRASHED. I went to my hotel room and fell asleep immediately. It had been some rough days with very little sleep, and now I knew I couldn't do it anymore. I had so many texts from my children, but I couldn't even focus on them properly. My eyes were so blurry from the lack of sleep that I couldn't even read them. They would have to wait.

Just an hour.

Three hours later, I woke up with drool on my cheek and feeling completely groggy. I looked at my phone, blinking my eyes to better be able to see. I opened the first text from Olivia when there was a knock on my door.

I opened it, then suddenly felt extremely self-conscious.

It was Alexander Huxley.

"Wow," he said with a handsome grin. He had the brown messenger bag swung over his shoulder as usual. "Rough night?"

"Fun," I said with a grimace. "What the heck are you doing here?"

"Writing my story, of course," he said. "Can I come in?"

I ran a hand through my hair, trying to correct my bangs.

"I won't bite. I promise," he added. "Unless you like that."

"I don't have anything for you, and you know it."

"I might have something for you, though," he said. "I think you'll want to hear me out."

I looked up, and my eyes met his. He seemed genuine and serious. It just got interesting.

"Come on in."

He followed me inside and sat down in the chair by the window. I pointed at the bathroom door.

"Just give me a sec to…."

He grinned again. "Fix yourself up a little? Yeah, you might need a little more than just a second."

I sent him a sarcastic smile. "This is fun."

I rushed to the bathroom and washed my face, then stared at myself in the mirror, thinking this was an impossible task. I brushed my hair and put it in a ponytail, then corrected the clothes I was still wearing from the night before. I smelled my armpit. It wasn't good. I applied some deodorant and hoped that would handle the worst of it. I would have to shower later when he was gone.

I decided it would have to do, then glanced at my phone and finally read the messages from my daughter. They were all about her needing money for an outfit for prom, and I realized I had forgotten to transfer it. I opened my bank app, then transferred money for her, titling it *Beautiful dress for prom*, then closed my phone and walked out into the room.

Alex had put some papers on the small table and looked up as I walked out.

"You can take a little extra time if you want," he said. "You seem like you rushed it a little."

"I really hope this is good," I said, then sat in the chair across from him, trying not to get too close in case he might smell me.

"What have you got?

"It's about Linda Smalls."

Part V

Ten hours later

Chapter 54

HER FEET WERE KILLING HER. It was all the extra weight she was placing on them constantly. It was exhausting. Senator Hartnett got into the elevator at the hotel where the conference was being held.

"You have an eight o'clock in the morning," her assistant Laura said. She was a short woman with thick brown hair who barely ever looked up from her iPad, where she kept Hartnett's entire schedule and life.

"Followed by a ten o'clock at the office, and then lunch with Senator Kelsey downtown at one, but you can't let that run too long. You know how much he talks, but you have to be at the budget meeting at two, so keep him on a short leash. He is expected to want you to vote for his climate tax reform. You are, of course, opposed to that, but make sure you let him down easy because we need his vote for bill 567 next week."

Hartnett groaned and closed her eyes while rubbing her bulging stomach. Laura noticed and stopped talking.

"I guess you must be tired by now, huh? Are you in pain?"

Hartnett smiled. "No more than usual. Well, that's not true.

Today, it's been a little more than usual, actually. I feel the weight of the baby now and need some rest. My feet and my back are killing me. And I have this stabbing pain in the bottom of my stomach."

Hartnett groaned again and leaned forward as the elevator moved up. Laura looked at her, concerned.

"Do you want me to call someone? Your doctor?"

Hartnett sucked in air through her teeth, bending forward further. "No, no. I'm fine. I just...I just need to lie down."

"Okay, well, we're almost there," Laura said. "Just a few more floors."

The elevator dinged and opened the doors. Laura grabbed Hartnett's briefcase and let her lean on her shoulder as they walked. When they reached the door, Laura helped her swipe her hotel card and held the door for her as she walked in, still moaning lightly in pain.

"Baby isn't due for at least a month," she said, her voice shivering. "Do you think you might be in labor?"

Hartnett looked down at her, then forced a smile. Laura was so young and so easily distraught.

"It's okay," she said. "I'm going to be fine. I've gone through childbirth before."

Laura eased up. "That's right."

Then, her face grew dark.

"Any news?"

Hartnett looked down at her, pushing away the growing sadness. Then, she shook her head.

"I'm sure she'll call soon," Laura said and placed a hand on Hartnett's shoulder.

Hartnett smiled, trying to seem reassuring that, of course, she believed so too.

But she wasn't so sure anymore.

She touched her stomach with another groan, bending forward.

"Shall I call the doctor?" Laura asked.

"I think I'll call him myself," Hartnett said. "I'm sure he'll tell me that all I need is rest."

"Do you want me to stay with you? Just in case?"

Hartnett bit down on her lip, then shook her head. "No need to. I'll call the doctor now. Then, I'll call for you if I need help."

Laura looked at her, insecure. "You sure? I don't mind…."

"Yes. I'm sure. Go to your room and let me talk to the doctor on my own. I want the privacy, please."

"O-okay."

Laura left, and Hartnett waited until the heavy door slammed behind her. Then, she grabbed her phone and made the call.

"Doc? Senator Hartnett here. It's time."

Chapter 55

WE DROVE out of town in Alex's rental car. I called Walsh and told her to meet us there and bring Rivers and his team. After hours of frantic searching, we believed we had finally managed to locate Linda Smalls. Alex had told me he talked to her sister, and she had revealed that she was worried about Linda. She believed she might be doing something terrible. She told him that Linda had read the article he had written, and now Alex was concerned about what she was up to as well. We found out through her credit card statements that she had rented a cabin two hours south of DC, near Charlottesville, through Airbnb. This was on the same day as she had rented the car that she had been seen in when picking up Steve Melton, Sr. All this time, I had believed those two somehow knew one another, that she helped him escape. Now, I realized that wasn't the case.

I had been informed that the local police near the cabin had received a distress call the day before from someone who told them he had heard screaming from inside the cabin when he stopped to ask for directions. He had pondered for a long time whether or not to call the police, then finally done it. He worried that the woman who had opened the door was in danger. A local police officer had been to the cabin and knocked on the door, but no one opened it, so he left again.

"I really hope we're not too late," I said as Alex took a turn up the small mountain road. Lots of big trees, covered in snow, surrounded us, and it would have been a gorgeous sight had the circumstances been different.

Alex nodded. "Me too."

He had a different look in his eyes now. One I hadn't seen in them before.

"I will never forgive myself if she hurt him," he mumbled.

"You can't think like that," I said.

"It was my article. If I hadn't revealed his name…it was my stupid editor who said he wanted the name."

I nodded. "Listen, we can't change the past. What's done is done. But just remember that Linda Smalls is making the wrong choices now. Not you."

He drove up in front of the cabin and stopped the car outside. I hadn't wanted him to come, but he had insisted and said he wouldn't let me drive his car.

I placed a hand on the grip of my gun as he parked. A local police patrol was already waiting outside in the street. Behind us came the SWAT team and parked their vans. Rivers and his team got into position and surrounded the cabin. Alex watched, and I could tell he was nervous. We watched the SWAT team go in, and I placed a hand on his arm.

"Stay here, okay? It's the safest."

He nodded.

Rivers and the rest of the SWAT team disappeared into the cabin. I followed as soon as I received the all-clear signal. I walked into the foyer and met Rivers; he shook his head.

"No one is here."

"I had a feeling they were gone," I said, annoyed. I put the gun back in the holster then walked into the kitchen. It was obvious that someone had been staying here recently. There were dishes and used coffee cups in the sink and a bag of bread on the counter. I stared out the window at the snowy landscape, then wondered where Linda had gone.

"What are you up to now?" I asked when Rivers came up behind me.

"Ma'am. There's something you need to see."

Chapter 56

LINDA FLOORED THE ACCELERATOR. In the rearview mirror, she could see the blinking lights as more police cars drove to the cabin.

She smiled, then thought about Steve Melton, Sr. in the trunk. She had tied him up and used duct tape to cover his wounds, thinking it would stop the bleeding.

When the first police officer had come to the door, she realized it was time to leave. She had thought about leaving Steve in the cabin, or rather his body. But she wasn't ready to let him go just yet. He still had some suffering to do.

She drove up the hill, going deeper into the forested area. She had left her phone at the cabin, but luckily there was a GPS in the car she could use. She knew how the police could track your phone and couldn't risk it. She didn't need a phone anyway. Only Trent would call to say goodnight like he did every night. He was staying with her sister while Linda was out of town. When she said goodbye to him and kissed him, she knew she would never see him again. In some way, she believed he knew it too.

"Take good care of him," she had said to her sister, Emma. "Don't let him eat sugar before bedtime, and make sure he showers three times a week. Read to him every night before bedtime. He loves that."

Then, she had shed a tear. Her sister had told her she was being foolish, that, of course, the boy would be fine.

Then, Linda had lifted her gaze and met hers, and she knew too. Instantaneously, she knew Linda wasn't coming back. She was only doing what she had to. There was no way she could live on, knowing this man had hurt her daughter. It was all she could think of. Even though the police were onto him, she knew that he would probably somehow cheat the system and never get punished. She read the stories in the papers. She watched the crime shows on TV. Most of these scumbags got away with their crimes. They got themselves expensive lawyers, and then they were untouchable. The last thing she wanted was to see him walk out of court, grinning because he got away with it.

Raping her daughter.

Keeping her locked up.

The very thought made her furious again, and she angrily hit the steering wheel. No, he deserved everything he got. And she needed to make sure he wouldn't be able to do it to someone else. Never again.

Even if it meant she never saw her son and her sister again. Even if she were put away for life for it, then she would at least have peace of mind, knowing he would never touch another girl again.

It was a price worth paying.

Linda sniffled and cranked up the heat in the car. It was freezing outside, and her fingertips were feeling numb. She drove through the narrow roads, thinking she was outsmarting all of them.

Stupid good-for-nothing law enforcement.

She had even left a little surprise for them at the cabin. She was only sad that she wouldn't be around to see it when it happened.

Chapter 57

RIVERS TOOK me into the living room, where he pointed at the floor. A huge area of the wood was stained underneath a dining chair.

"Blood," I said.

He nodded. "And lots of it."

Someone had tried to wipe it up, and there were soaked towels in a pile next to the chair. I shook my head in disbelief.

"What on earth are you doing, Linda?"

"I've called the techs," Rivers said.

"Good," I said with a deep sigh. "We need to know whose blood it is, even though I have a pretty good idea."

"They should be here any minute."

I looked around, and on the dining table, I spotted a phone. I walked closer and looked down at it. From seeing the pink case, I guessed it belonged to a woman. It could be Linda's. If so, then this was important.

"We need this secured as well," I said.

"Techs are here," Rivers yelled from the other end of the living room. I watched as more people came into the house, wearing bodysuits and gloves. I made sure they secured the phone safely in an evidence bag. They took pictures of the bloody floors and dusted for fingerprints.

This process always made me feel helpless and restless. I wanted to get ahold of all the evidence and start putting the pieces together, but I had to wait for the professionals to do their work.

I stood for a little while, looking around, then stared at the breakfast counter and into the kitchen. I guessed that Linda had left a ton of fingerprints behind. She didn't occur to me to be the type who was rational enough to cover her tracks well. She was acting out of anger now and not thinking straight. She was in deep trouble. It made me sad to think about. How could she have gone so far? What went on in that head of hers? I wasn't exactly fond of the woman after what happened at the soccer field, but still. I couldn't believe she was this engulfed by the thirst for revenge.

I returned to the kitchen, and my eyes fell on the beautiful white gas stove. It looked like it was from the fifties, and it was gorgeous. But something was wrong. It took me a few seconds to figure out what exactly it was.

A faint hissing sound. A vague odor of rotten eggs.

Then, my heart stopped. I was staring right at it.

The stove. One of the knobs was turned.

Oh, dear Lord! She left one of the burners open when she left, leaking gas into the house.

I jerked my head to the side, but it felt like a dream—like it turned way too slow. My eyes fell on all the people in the living room, walking in and out—serious eyes, hard at work. And then I saw a guy approach the wall between the kitchen and living room, raising his hand toward the light switch.

Going to turn it on.

I opened my mouth to scream, to stop him, but no sound left my lips. It was like I didn't have enough air in my lungs.

LITTLE DID SHE KNOW

It was too late.
He flipped it.

Chapter 58

THEN:

"We're not getting anywhere."

Detective Brent exhaled deeply. He placed his head between his hands and shook it.

"We've interrogated the dad over and over, but he refuses to give in. It's been three weeks now since baby Anna disappeared. We have even searched their entire property and had the dogs out to see if he buried her in the back yard, but nothing. We had divers out in the lake behind the house, searching through it, inch by inch, combing the darn waterhole for anything that could help us. Nothing."

Brent paused to sip his coffee. Garcia sat at the desk next to his. They had been going through the case files one more time to see if there was anything, a detail maybe, that they might have missed.

"Dang it," Brent said and slammed his fist into the desk. "I know he did something to that kid. I just know it. I see it in his eyes."

"Do you want to get him in here again for another talk?" Garcia asked.

Brent leaned back in his office chair. His back had been killing him lately, and his wife was bugging him to see a chiropractor. But he didn't want to. They couldn't do anything anyway, and he'd had this lower back pain since he was in his early forties. It wasn't getting worse except when he was under a lot of stress and pressure—like now. Plus, he didn't really believe in chiropractors. They weren't even real doctors. They just wanted his money.

They were all crooks.

"Nah, he'll just say the same things he did all the other times. And then he'll ask for his lawyer if we start asking more questions. It's no use."

"And the wife?"

"I don't think she knows anything. Or I'd say she's a really good actress. She seems completely oblivious to the fact that her husband might have hurt their child."

"He's never harmed the child before," Garcia said, fiddling with his steaming coffee cup. It annoyed Brent that he did that. Just like when he tapped his pen on the desk to some rhythm all day.

"So, she says," Brent said. "She might be lying to protect him. Or she could be scared of him. He might have threatened her to silence, to lie for him. Or he may have hurt the kid before, and she just never saw it."

Garcia wrinkled his forehead. "Wouldn't a mom see the bruises?"

Brent shrugged. "Maybe. Who knows? All I do know is that I somehow need to break him. I just don't know how."

"And find the baby," Garcia said. "Don't forget that."

"I don't think the baby is alive, I am afraid," Brent said, heavy at heart.

Garcia's eyes got distant, and he nodded. They both knew the likelihood was small. It saddened them, and they sat in silence for a few minutes when the phone on Garcia's desk rang. He picked it up, then went quiet.

Brent looked at his partner with bated breath. Something was up.

"Yes, yes. Okay."

Garcia hung up. He looked spooked.

"What's wrong?" Brent asked.

"They…they…you won't believe this. They found her."

"Excuse me?"

He swallowed and repeated it.

"They found the baby. Or rather they found *a* baby, but they think it might be Anna."

Chapter 59

I FELT the explosion first in my chest—like an extreme force hit me there and reverberated through my body—like a punch, but just a lot more forceful. Second, I felt it in my head—like my brain was being slammed against my skull. It all went so fast that I didn't see anything, nor did I hear anything. People will tell you it's thunderous, but I didn't hear anything at all. I did feel the push, though, and felt how I was propelled through the door. The cement block wall shattered, and I was blown against the living room wall, along with all the debris. I was sure the house was about to collapse, and for a few seconds, I was sure I would die.

Then, something changed. About ten to fifteen feet away, I could make out a doorway through the dust and falling debris. I panicked. Seeing the opening gave me hope, and I switched into survival mode. I was climbing over the debris while it was literally still falling, dust filling my mouth and lungs.

Somehow, I managed to make it outside and crawl about a hundred feet away before I collapsed.

The next thing I remember was hearing voices and feeling

hands on my body. I didn't feel any pain until I was about halfway to the hospital. Then, it struck, and I woke up in a scream. A hand found mine, and I heard Alex's voice somewhere in the distance.

"You need to lie still, Eva Rae. We're almost there."

The pain shot through my body, and it felt like my skin would peel off. I was wrapped in foil blankets, and voices were yelling things around me that I couldn't grasp. I tried to open my eyes but had to close them again since it was too painful.

I felt my body move as I was taken out of the ambulance and rushed through the hospital's hallways. Every now and then, I would open my eyes and see the lights above rushing by and faces looking down at me. There were questions asked, but I couldn't answer.

I was taken to the burn center, where new faces took over, and my body was inspected. I was in pain, and somehow, I managed to communicate that, so they gave me more morphine. There was so much going on that I could barely understand what had happened. I felt so confused; I couldn't even say my own name. Faces, hands, and voices surrounded me in turbulent chaos that I wanted badly to escape but couldn't.

I prayed that I would pass out. I wanted to. I was in so much pain; I just wanted to die or at least lose consciousness.

But for some reason, I didn't.

Instead, I experienced everything they did to me in a strange haze of pain and confusion.

"What happened?" was the first thing I managed to say at one point.

A set of eyes looked down at me from above. She looked kind and compassionate but also worried.

"There was an explosion," her high-pitched voice said, cutting through my foggy brain. "You were lucky."

Lucky? This is lucky?

I wanted to scream this at her, but there wasn't enough air in my scorched lungs to say more. The extra morphine was beginning to kick in, and I felt numb. I also felt drowsy. Not enough to fall asleep since there was still too much pain, but enough to no longer care.

Chapter 60

SHE TURNED the faucet and let the water flow into the tub. Senator Hartnett felt the water coming out and turned it to get hotter. She liked her bathtubs warm, and she had been freezing all day. Getting her body sunk into the water should warm her up.

And maybe remove some of the stress she felt.

Senator Hartnett massaged her neck. It was so sore and stiff. Her entire back was complaining about the extra weight it had been carrying around. She was really looking forward to it being over and actually didn't mind that it was happening a little earlier than expected.

She had told the doctor that her contractions had started. But she also knew there was no rush. Her first baby took thirty-six hours to get out, she told him. It would be faster this time, of course, but the contractions were still light and far apart so far. And her water hadn't broken yet. There was still plenty of time.

But it had begun.

"I'll be right over," Dr. Holden had said. "I'm bringing my midwife."

Hartnett had planned a home birth from the moment she

knew she was having a baby and paid Dr. Holden to be on standby for when it happened. She wanted to give birth in the comfort of her own home, so she had her husband come pick her up at the hotel where she was staying for the conference. He had taken her home and helped her get upstairs to the bathroom, so she could get in the tub. The doctor said that the warm water would help with the contractions until the midwife got there with the birthing tub they had planned to set up in the living room downstairs.

She was glad she was missing out on the hectic birth at a hospital like last time. It had been more than chaotic and, if she were honest, a little traumatic. The doctor had been hesitant at first when she told him her plans. He wouldn't recommend her giving birth at home since they would be far away from the hospital if something went wrong. Besides, he said, she had to remember that it was many years ago that she gave birth last, and a lot had changed. But she had argued that, yes, it was many years ago since her daughter was now a teenager, and a lot could have changed at the hospitals, but she just wasn't willing to take the chance. Besides, she was a public figure now, and if anyone at the hospital couldn't keep their mouth shut, the press would be all over the hospital after only a few minutes. And she didn't want to have to deal with that on top of going through a birth. She simply refused to.

No, she argued that a birth in the comfort of her home was the way she wanted to do it. She paid Dr. Holden a huge sum of money to keep her happy and to keep quiet, so he'd better agree with her.

And that was the end of that discussion. He promised he would do his best to make things as smooth as possible. And now, the time had come for him to show up for her.

Senator Hartnett felt the water again as it was filling up and was happy to realize it felt very comfortable. The temperature was just right. Her back was killing her, and the water would help loosen up the muscles.

"You almost ready?"

Hartnett looked up and met her husband's eyes, then smiled before turning off the faucet. She nodded, feeling excited.

"Let's do this. I can't wait."

She rose to her feet and lifted her arms in the air. "Can you help me with this?"

Her husband stepped forward then helped pull her shirt over her head, revealing her big stomach underneath it. Then she turned around and let him help her detach it in the back. He loosened the straps, then pulled it off and placed the silicone pregnancy belly on the chair next to the bath.

Senator Hartnett stretched, then moved her shoulders, feeling free.

"Oh, thank you. That feels nice. I'm not gonna miss wearing that thing; that's for sure. Make sure it's put away before people get here."

"Of course," he said as he grabbed the fake pregnancy belly and put it in a closet by the end wall. He closed the door and then helped Senator Hartnett slide her slim naked body into the warm water.

She closed her eyes with a deep sigh.

"All right," she said and looked up at her husband. "It's showtime."

Chapter 61

"YOU **WERE** LUCKY."

I stared at Alexander, who was standing by my bedside. Then, I looked down at my body. I had second-degree burns on my legs and arms, they had told me. And then they kept repeating the same words over and over again.

"You were lucky."

I didn't believe them. It didn't feel like any kind of luck. I told Alex this when I finally felt better and realized he was sleeping in my room, sitting slumped over in a chair.

"How can you say that?" I asked. "Look at me."

"Because most of the people who were in the house with you were way more severely injured."

"Really?"

His eyes were so serious that it frightened me. It wasn't like Alex to be so somber.

"Walsh? What happened to her?" I asked, slightly panicking.

"Walsh is fine. She was outside at the time of the explosion. But we still don't know if Rivers is going to make it," he said. "The chimney fell on him when the cabin collapsed. They managed to bring him back to life at the scene, but he's been in a coma since he was brought in. You, Eva Rae Thomas, were the luckiest one of them all. You got off easy. You got some burns and some bumps and bruises, but that is all."

That shut me off. I didn't know everyone else was in such a bad state. It also made me feel incredibly guilty. Because, why me? Why was I so lucky, like they said?

"I just don't understand," I said. "I was in the kitchen. I was closest to the explosion. Why were the others worse off than me?"

"They say it was because you were at the center of the blast. Like the eye of the storm, you know? As gas explodes, it produces a powerful shockwave that surges away from the ignition point. This blast and the heat radiated from the combusting gas are the things to avoid if you want to survive an explosion. The massive blast pushed everything in the surrounding area, even the trees outside were flattened, and the cabin collapsed. I even felt the explosion while sitting in the car outside. It was like the car was lifted off the ground for a few seconds. A window was blown in; there was glass everywhere. I saw you crawling out of the collapsing building a few seconds later. It was surreal."

I stared at him, mouth gaping, then smiled. "They told me you did CPR on me; thanks for that."

He blushed. "Ah, don't flatter yourself. I did what any decent man would have done. You weren't breathing. I had to save your life, right? How else am I going to keep writing this story? I need you to solve this case for me, so I can write an amazing piece about it."

"Of course," I said. "It's always about the story."

He threw out his hands, his eyes avoiding mine.

"That's what makes me such an excellent reporter."

"Now you're the one flattering yourself," I said and looked at the TV screen on the wall behind him.

"Could you turn this up for me? I want to hear it."

Part VI

Chapter 62

HER HANDS WERE SHAKING, and she couldn't make them stop. Linda squeezed the steering wheel so tightly that her knuckles were turning white. Yet, she was still shaking. The shaking made its way through her arms and into her torso; soon, she had to let go of the wheel and hide her face in her hands.

Things had gotten out of hand. Linda wasn't sure she could control it anymore. The explosion at the cabin had been bigger than anything she had imagined. She had been sitting in her car up the road from the cabin when it happened. It had been so powerful that she had felt it shake her vehicle. And that was when she got frightened—when she looked out the window and saw the pillar of smoke coming up from the area between the trees.

I caused that. Holy moly!

It was bigger than she had thought it would be, and now there were a lot of cops in the hospital, one of them fighting for his life, they said on the TV at the gas station right outside of Charlottesville, where she stopped for gas and snacks. Then they had also shown pictures of her and Steve Melton, Sr., and said to contact local police if anyone saw them. She had pulled the hoodie up over her face while watching it and paying the cashier for her chips and sodas in cash. The cashier didn't seem to realize anything but just kept looking at his phone.

That was when they had said that Steve Melton, Sr. was no longer a suspect in the case of the missing baby Desiree and the kidnapping of Clarissa Smalls, who showed up in Florida recently.

Linda stared at the screen behind the tall cashier guy with the long hair in dreadlocks. She couldn't believe what she was hearing.

Steve Melton was innocent?

How is that possible?

Now, she was in the parked car, slamming her hands against the wheel. It had all been for nothing? She had shot a guy twice, for what? Nothing? He was innocent?

Oh, dear God.

What have I done?

She started the car back up and left the parking lot in front of the gas station, then took off onto the road. She had checked on Steve in the trunk earlier, and he was in a bad state. He had lost so much blood that he wasn't even conscious anymore. He needed help.

What do I do?

She stepped on the accelerator and pressed the Toyota to its max. She had to get out of here fast. She drove for a few minutes, then spotted a CVS and drove into the parking lot. She hurried inside the sliding doors and approached the smiling lady behind the counter, who was wearing way too much make-up for Linda's taste.

"Can I help you?"

"I need to find a hospital," she said. "Fast."

The woman's face grew serious, and her smile froze.

"It's an emergency," Linda added.

"Yes, yes, of course," the woman replied. "There's the University

Hospital in downtown Charlottesville. They have an ER. Do you know where that is?"

"If I knew anything about this area, I wouldn't be asking you for directions right now."

She was panting, agitated, and gesticulating so much that the woman recoiled.

"O-okay, well, just continue down the expressway for about ten or fifteen minutes, and then turn right at the intersection by Jefferson Park Avenue. You can't miss it."

Chapter 63

ALEX TURNED up the television sound, and I listened to the story they were telling. The image I was looking at, the one that had made me react and ask him to turn up the sound, was an old still photo of a man in his early thirties.

"This is the latest picture that we have of her husband," the anchor said to his expert in the studio. "It's from 2006, right? That's a long time ago."

"Yes, he has always been a very private man and stayed out of the public eye," the expert said. "In many ways, they are a very modern family. She's the working mom who brings home the money while he stays at home with the children. Well, so far, it has only been their one child, their daughter, whom they have managed to keep completely out of the media spotlight as well, to give her an ordinary childhood growing up in Kansas, where Hartnett was elected. But now, soon, they will have another one, we suspect."

"And for those viewers who are just joining us now," the anchor said, looking into the camera, "we can say that we have just received breaking news that Senator Hartnett has gone into labor.

It's a little early, so we do hope there won't be complications and that the baby is healthy. With me here, I have political expert Jane Roslin who has followed Hartnett's career closely for many years."

He turned to face her again. "And tell me, Jane, how does this little family plan on making the everyday work? Because Hartnett is a very busy woman. Will it be the husband who takes care of the baby once again?"

"Yes, that is what we must assume. They have an entirely unique family constellation that we can all learn a lot from. It is actually possible for the man to stay at home and the woman to have a career. It's very inspiring, I must say. But again, I must add that we don't know for sure that she is giving birth yet. We only know there's a rumor about it and that the senator has canceled all her meetings for the rest of the week, which is highly unusual for the hardworking Hartnett."

"Thank you, Jane. We'll get back to this news as soon as we know more. Now, to Russia. The Russian minister Igev Krav…"

I muted the TV with the remote Alex had given me. I stared at him, heart pounding in my chest.

"What's going on?" he asked. "I don't like the look in your eyes."

I was biting my lip. Suddenly, the drowsiness was gone, but so was the pain. I reached over and grabbed my phone, then called my dad.

"If I give you an address, can you find out who owns the house?" I asked. "It should be easy."

He accepted the task, and I hung up. Alex was still looking at me. "What are you up to?"

"The picture," I said. "The man in the photo. I know him."

"Hartnett's husband?"

I nodded. "He's the guy who was in the car with Steve Melton, Jr. He was the one who picked him up at his condo and drove him to the retired pediatrician, Dr. Green."

"Okay? But w-what does this mean? I don't understand? And

what is that about the address? Why didn't you get FBI's people to find the name?"

I sat up in bed and looked at my phone like I thought it would go so quickly that he would already be getting back to me. I wasn't wrong.

"Because my dad is way faster than any of them."

I showed Alex the phone, which was now ringing with my dad's name on the display.

Chapter 64

THEN:

"This almost never happens, so I want you to prepare for the fact that it might not be her."

Detective Brent looked at Amelia as he helped her out of the car. A patrol had picked her up at her house while Brent and Garcia went to get the baby.

Amelia looked back at him, her eyes filling. "But there's a possibility it might be her?"

Brent sighed and closed the car door behind her. He didn't really know what to say to that. In his many years as a detective, missing children usually never turned up this late after they were kidnapped or taken—at least not alive. Usually, they ended up finding them, well…dead. This was highly unusual, and it made Brent slightly uncomfortable.

"I just want you to be prepared for the fact that it might not be her," he said.

She nodded, and they walked to the entrance of the police station. He held the door for her.

"Where did they find her?" she asked as she passed him.

"At the mall," Brent said and closed the glass door behind him. "She was in a car seat, and a local security guard passed her on his rounds. He couldn't find her parents anywhere, and after a while, with no one claiming her, he took her to his office, where he checked the security cameras. Unfortunately, there was a blind spot right where she was placed, so he couldn't see who had left her there. Then, he called the police."

"At the mall? I can't believe it," Amelia said while her voice was trembling with excitement.

It worried Brent deeply. He didn't want her to get her hopes up.

"I know. It's quite…well, I don't know what to call it, to be honest. But let's keep calm now. Like I said. This never happens. I have never…in my twenty-five years on the job had this happen before."

Amelia stopped and sent him a look. "That doesn't mean it can't happen. Don't you believe in miracles, Detective Brent?"

He forced a smile. "It's hard to do with the kind of messed up stuff that I see every day. But I'm a cynic like most cops, so…."

"I'm not a cynic. I believe in the impossible," Amelia said. "And I'm a cop too, remember?"

He placed a hand on her skinny shoulder. She seemed so fragile. Gosh, how he hoped this was her baby.

"How could I forget? This way."

He held the door for her again, and they walked into the main office. Garcia had taken the baby to the captain's office, and she was entertaining her. She had a little one at home herself, and they had just been told she was pregnant again. That was why she had felt so sick lately.

Brent knocked, and the captain yelled for them to come in. Brent opened the door and found Garcia on the other side of it. Both he and the captain were staring into the car seat on the desk with the tiny baby cooing inside it. She was tiny but had big blue eyes that stared up at them as they stepped closer. Amelia stared down into the car seat, then stood as if she were frozen for a few seconds. Then, her shoulders slumped, and Brent felt his heart drop.

Chapter 65

I WAS STARING at my notes. I had Alex give me his notepad from his messenger bag and a pen to write down what my dad told me. I listened to what he said, then had him repeat it twice—just to be completely sure I had heard him right.

Then I hung up and looked at Alex.

"Are you going to tell me what's going on?" he asked, throwing out his hands. "You look like you've seen a ghost. You're not usually this pale. Not even when you're in a hospital bed."

I was barely blinking. There were so many thoughts rushing through my mind. I could hardly believe the conclusion I had come to, so I tried to fit the pieces together, again and again, hoping for a different result, but they still painted the same picture.

"I can't believe it."

"What can't you believe?" he asked. "Can you throw a man a bone here?"

I removed the covers then pulled out my drip. "I don't have time for that. I need to go. Now."

Alex stepped forward. "Hey, you can't do that. You're…"

I looked up at him. "And who is going to stop me? You?"

"But don't you need to...at least talk to a doctor? Let me call for a nurse and ask them if it's...."

"I don't have time for that," I said. "Do you have my clothes?"

Alex nodded. "I brought your suitcase from the hotel."

I slid down from the bed, then rushed to the suitcase leaning up against the wall. I opened it, then started to pull out a pair of loose sweatpants and a baggy T-shirt. I found underwear and then took off my hospital gown, wincing in pain. Putting on clothes with second-degree burns on your body was more painful than I thought.

"Whoa," Alex said.

"Cover your eyes," I said, "if you can't take it."

"I wouldn't necessarily say that," he said with a goofy smile. "I mean, you...you're...really...I was just taken by surprise, is all. Usually, I have to take a girl out to dinner before she takes off her clothes for me."

I sent him a look, and he turned around. I got dressed while Alex turned his back to me. I couldn't really care about him right now. This was too important, and I had to hurry.

When I was done, I walked to him, grabbed my phone, then grabbed my wallet, gun, and badge from the locker where the nurses had put them.

"You have your car, right?"

"Yes. I rode here in the ambulance with you, but I went back and got it yesterday. It has a smashed window.

"But it's driveable, right?"

He nodded.

"Hand me the keys," I said and stretched out my hand.

He pulled back.

"No way."

"I need it. It's urgent."

"I understand that, but up until a few seconds ago, you were in a hospital bed being treated for burns and a severe concussion. There is no way I am letting you drive out somewhere on your own."

I rolled my eyes. I didn't have time to argue with this guy.

"At least let me drive you," he said.

I groaned, annoyed, then started to walk out into the hallway, looking for the elevator.

"All right. If you can keep up."

Chapter 66

LINDA DROVE up in front of the ER then parked the car. She then rushed to the back and pulled Steve out from the back seat, where she had put him after talking to the lady at CVS. He was still unconscious but breathing. She had checked for his pulse and was relieved when she found one.

Now, she was dragging him out of the car, and he landed on the asphalt below. Two men came running out of the ER, pulling a stretcher.

"I found this guy lying in the street and drove him here," she said, hoping they'd buy into her little lie.

The two men looked at her, then down at Steve Melton on the ground.

"Looks like he's been shot," she added. "Twice. But he has a pulse. I checked when I got him into my car. He's not dead."

She felt how badly her voice was trembling as she spoke. The two men didn't seem to care much about her. Instead, they focused on Steve. They lifted him onto the stretcher. Linda stared at Steve, her heart beating relentlessly in her chest.

What have I done? What on earth have I done!

"Stay here," one of the men said as they were about to take him away. "You need to talk to the police when they get here. You can wait inside."

Linda nodded in agreement, but as soon as she watched them rush Steve away, she turned on her heel and walked back to her car. She got in, then stepped on the accelerator and drove away.

"No way I am talking to no police," she mumbled inside the car as she drove around the building, hoping she would manage to get away. She knew there were probably cameras everywhere, but she was already a sought-after person, so she'd just have to get out of the state quickly.

If this guy didn't take Clarissa, then who did?

Just as she asked herself that question, she looked out the window. She was passing the hospital's main entrance just as someone else was coming out of there.

Linda hit the brakes.

She stared at the two people walking across the parking lot, barely believing her own eyes.

"What the...what is *she* doing here?"

Her eyes followed Eva Rae Thomas as she—together with that stupid journalist who had interviewed Linda right after Clarissa came back and asked all those annoying questions—was striding across the parking lot and stopped at a car that had a shattered window.

"What are you doing here, Eva Rae?" she said again while watching her get into the passenger seat of the car with the missing window. The journalist got into the driver's seat and started up the car.

Linda watched them closely as they backed out and took off. She stared at the car as it came to a complete stop at the end of the parking lot. They took a right turn, and Linda glared at them. Then, she hit the accelerator and followed.

"But more importantly, where are you going?"

Chapter 67

WHEN DR. HOLDEN arrived at the house, Senator Hartnett was sitting on the bed in the bedroom, holding the baby in her arms. Her husband let the doctor in and looked at him with worried eyes.

"You're late. The baby has already arrived."

The doctor looked surprised.

"Really? I didn't take that long."

The husband shrugged. "The baby came fast this time. Not like last time when it took forever."

"I should call off the midwife, then," Dr. Holden said. "How are they? Mother and baby?"

The husband closed the door, then looked at him, concerned. "Mother is doing just fine, but we're not so sure about the baby."

"What's wrong with the baby?" Dr. Holden asked.

The husband signaled for him to follow him up the stairs, walking toward the bedroom.

"Something seems to be wrong with her."

Dr. Holden nodded, walking behind the husband up the stairs. "Ah, can you say more?"

"She's not crying," he continued. "My wife gave birth inside the water, but the girl didn't scream when we pulled her out. She hasn't made any noises but is just sleeping and breathing raggedly."

"That's odd," Dr. Holden said, walking faster behind the husband. They reached the door to the bedroom, and the husband opened it.

"We're so glad you're here. We feel helpless."

"That's understandable," he said and walked inside.

Senator Hartnett was sitting on the bed, wearing a bathrobe, her hair still wet. She was holding a small bundle in her arms that could only be the infant.

"She's probably small since she was born premature," the doctor said and approached her. "That might be it. We can take her to the hospital and make sure she gets the care that other premature children get."

He sat on the edge of the bed. Senator Hartnett didn't look up. She kept staring at the baby in her arms.

"Can I take a look?" Dr. Holden asked.

She looked at him like he was asking to take the baby from her and never give it back.

"I need to listen to her heart," he explained.

Senator Hartnett eased up; then, she nodded with a sniffle. "She's so quiet. I fear something is wrong."

"We'll figure out what it is," he said and placed his stethoscope on the baby's heart when Senator Hartnett opened her arms just enough for him to do so. He gave her a serious look.

"What's wrong, Doctor? What's wrong with my baby?"

"I'm afraid her heart isn't beating the way it's supposed to. We need to get her to the hospital. Can I just hold her for a second?"

He reached in and grabbed the tiny baby, then pulled it out from between the senator's hands. Senator Hartnett protested, but he took her anyway and examined her.

He looked first at the senator, then at the husband.

"What's going on here?"

"What do you mean?" Senator Hartnett asked.

Dr. Holden shook his head. "This baby wasn't just born. She's older, even though she is tiny. I know this child. She's the…."

He didn't get to finish his sentence before he felt the cold steel of a gun pressed against his temple. The husband leaned down toward him and said, "No, she isn't. Do we agree?"

"Y-yes."

"Good. Smart choice. Now, save her life."

Chapter 68

"I CAN'T BELIEVE IT."

Alex didn't look at me. He kept his eyes on the road ahead, and I was quite thankful for that. He was speeding through downtown, and frankly, not a very good driver. He drove up behind a red truck and barely stopped in time.

"What the heck? Did you see this idiot?"

I covered my eyes and screamed, thinking we would slam into the truck. But Alex hit the brakes just in time, and I looked at him while he cursed at the truck's driver. Then, he honked the horn before turning the wheel into the emergency lane and driving past him. He then swung the car back into the road and hit the accelerator again. Meanwhile, I grabbed onto the handle, clutching it tightly like my grandmother used to do, terrified that this was my last moment on this earth.

"What did you say?" he asked when we came to an area that had less traffic. I finally breathed a little easier but didn't dare let go of the handle.

"What's that?"

"You said you couldn't believe it. What can't you believe?" Alex asked.

I shook my head. "Just that it's been right in front of me all this time, and I didn't see it. Turn right here."

He did but had too much speed, and the car skidded sideways. I held onto the handle with both hands. Alex got the car back on the road, then accelerated, throwing me forward.

"You still haven't told me what we're doing," he said.

I exhaled, relieved when I saw that we were almost there.

"It's at the end of this street," I said and pointed at the house. "The two-story yellow one."

"Why this house?" he asked while going way too fast through this nice family-oriented neighborhood. A house had a sign out in front, saying:

DRIVE LIKE YOUR KIDS LIVE HERE

"What's here?" he continued.

"I don't know yet. So far, it's just a hunch," I said.

"It's for sale?" he asked as he drove the car up on the pavement and came to a sudden halt, throwing me forward.

"Yes, and that's what threw me off last time I was here."

"What do you mean? You've been here before?"

I sighed and looked at the house. There was a car in the driveway. It hadn't been there the last time.

"Yes, we didn't find anything then. But I have a feeling it was right there in front of us."

I opened the car door and got out. Alex yelled after me, "What was? What was in front of you all this time?"

I didn't respond but slammed the door shut and started to walk up toward the house. Alex stepped out and followed me.

"Can't you tell me anything? Anything at all?"

I paused in front of the door, trying to think through my next move. Should I call for backup? But what if I was wrong? Plus, if the baby was in there, as I suspected, she probably didn't have time to wait for backup to arrive. She needed to be taken to a hospital.

If, in fact, she was still alive.

There was no knowing at this point. All I had was my hope.

"Hello? At least give me something?"

I looked up at him.

"Whose house is this?" he asked.

"The oil company Telp Industries own this house. They recently filed for bankruptcy, and that's why it's for sale."

I paused and saw the confusion on his face, then knocked on the door.

"Telp Industries is Senator Hartnett's father's company, and this is where she stays with her family. She is required to have an address in Kansas, where she was elected, but she spends most of her time here in Washington, DC. Putting it in her father's company's name makes it harder for the media to find them, and they get to live quietly. But that's how Clarissa got her driver's license at only fourteen. Kansas is one of the states that allows you to get your license at fourteen. She had an address in Kansas but lived most of her life in DC because her mom, or the woman she knew as her mom, was a senator."

Alex stared at me, baffled.

"Clarissa Smalls? But…how?"

Chapter 69

THEN:

Brent couldn't help himself. He wanted so badly to comfort Amelia. Seeing the disappointment on her face made him almost lose it. He had so hoped it was her child. He wanted her to get her baby back so badly.

He placed a comforting hand on her shoulder.

"I'm truly sorr...."

A squeal coming from the woman in front of him caused him to remove his hand from her shoulder. He looked at her as she clasped her mouth, tears springing to her eyes.

"Oh, my God," she said with a high-pitched voice. "It's her. It's really her. I can barely believe my own eyes. It's her!"

"It is? Really?" Brent asked, quite dumbfounded. From her first reaction, he had been so certain it wasn't her baby.

"It is! It's my baby. This is Anna Catherine Hartnett. We call her Anna or sometimes Cate."

Brent looked inside the car seat. He had to admit the child looked just like the pictures, but then again, he thought all newborns looked alike.

"And you're certain of this?" Garcia asked, looking happily at Brent and their captain. Everyone in the office was smiling, even Brent.

She nodded.

"Yes, yes, oh, God yes, this is my baby. I thought I would never see her again. You have no idea how grateful I am to you, all of you."

There was a light knock on the door, and someone opened it. An officer came in with the husband, Ron. His eyes were red, and he looked like he had lost a lot of weight. His eyes met those of his wife and filled with tears.

"Come see, Ron," Amelia said.

"Is it...is it...?" he looked confused at all their faces, then hurried to the car seat and peeked inside. Then he burst into tears.

"Oh, thank God!"

He started to cry. His wife grabbed him, and they hugged, both while crying. He looked at the captain.

"Can I...?"

She nodded, on the verge of tears herself. Ron bent down and took baby Anna in his hands. With a deep exhale, he held her tight to his chest, closing his eyes. His wife kissed the baby's head while crying still, then caressed her head gently.

"Oh, dear God," Ron repeated. "How I missed this. Just the smell of her head alone when you kiss her."

"It is the best smell in the world," the captain said, her voice cracking, fighting her own tears. She touched her stomach gently, and Brent remembered that she was pregnant.

"Do we know what happened to her?" Ron asked with a sniffle, looking at Brent. "Who took her?"

Brent shook his head. "To be honest, we don't. The kidnapper might have regretted taking her. Maybe taking care of an infant proved to be harder than he thought; maybe he just wanted to scare you, or maybe he got spooked himself. Maybe he wanted to press you for money but then regretted it."

"We had a doctor check her out, and she is in perfect health," the captain added. "She's been well fed and taken care of. The important part is that she is back with her family now. We will, of course, still investigate and chase down the sick bastard who took her, but for now, I say you take your baby home and enjoy every moment with her. We will need to make a DNA match to be certain that she is actually your child, but that is just a formality."

"Of course," Amelia Hartnett said while putting baby Anna back in the car seat.

Ron grabbed the handle and said as they left, "We're just happy that we got her back. We will be eternally grateful to you all for bringing us together as a family again."

Chapter 70

"AMELIA HARTNETT?"

Alex stared at me, barely blinking.

"As in Senator Hartnett? Are you kidding me?"

I shook my head while knocking again.

"You're telling me Senator Hartnett stole Clarissa Smalls?" he continued. "That she took her from the hospital in Florida fourteen years ago when she was just a few hours old? Then brought her back here and raised her as her own?"

"I'm afraid so. See, her own baby was stolen in the middle of the night by a kidnapper, and for weeks, the police searched for her everywhere but didn't find her. The detectives on the case had their eyes on the father, her husband Ron, and kept pushing him as a suspect. Meanwhile, she became desperate. Thinking she would never see her baby again, she went to Florida and stole another baby, then brought her back here and placed her in a car seat at the local mall, where a security guard found her. The local DC police thought it had to be the Hartnett baby because she had gone missing, and then when they called in the couple to see this baby, they said it was theirs, even though it wasn't. Amelia used to be a cop. She knew how it would go down. No one doubted her since she was one of their own. They must have paid off someone to get the DNA tests to match because I strictly remember it coming back as a match. That's the only explanation I can come up with. Amelia comes from oil money, so she could have done that."

Alex wrinkled his forehead. "What do you mean you remember?"

I took a deep breath and met his eyes. Then, he realized it.

"You were on the case!"

I nodded, feeling heavy with guilt. I wasn't glad to have to admit to this.

"I was the commanding officer on the case. It was before my time in the FBI. I was still young and dreamed of climbing the ladder. I was so happy when they made me captain for the detective division and the investigative unit for a brief period. My predecessor beat up his wife and ended up doing jail time for domestic disputes. But I was also pregnant and in over my head. I had a young child at home and a failing marriage, and I was pregnant with my second child. I was sick most days, throwing up and feeling awful. I had a huge caseload to oversee, and it was all very chaotic. Not that that is any excuse. I didn't do my job very well. All I wanted was for them to get their baby back. I was so relieved that I never suspected anything could be wrong. We all wanted it to be their baby and to be able to sleep again. When I saw Ron's face in the car driving with Steve Melton, Jr., I knew I had seen him before, and then I saw the same face on the TV screen when they talked about Hartnett's marriage and her going into early labor."

Alex's eyes grew wide. "You...you think...."

I nodded. "Yes. That's exactly what I think."

I knocked again, then yelled, "FBI, open the door, please."

When no answer came, I grabbed the doorknob and turned it. It was locked.

"I gotta get in there. Stand back."

I lifted my leg then kicked the door. It moved a little but didn't open. I tried again, and this time Alex helped. The door slammed open, and I signaled for Alex to stay behind me, then stepped in.

Chapter 71

"WHAT ON EARTH IS THAT?"

Amelia Hartnett gasped and looked at her husband. She had gotten dressed and was zipping her jeans when she heard it.

"Who is that at the front door, knocking?"

Ron shook his head. Dr. Holden was attending to the baby, desperately trying to keep her alive by massaging her chest with his fingers.

"Who IS that!" Amelia yelled at her husband. "Did you tell anyone we were here?"

"I don't know," Ron said.

"FBI, open up!" a voice sounded from downstairs.

Amelia's eyes met Ron's, and desperation set in.

"FBI? Ron? FBI?"

"I...I don't...."

"You led the FBI straight to our door!?"

He threw out his hands. "It's not like I did it on purpose. They must have followed me here."

Amelia pointed at him. "You had to go see that doctor. I told you not to. I specifically told you not to go see that pediatrician."

"What did you want me to do, huh? The baby was sick. I was desperate. I knew Steve knew someone who was a retired pediatrician. I remember he told me once when visiting Catherine. You know how that kid was always hanging out with us. I had to do something, and he was nice enough to agree to help me, despite everything that had happened."

"Ah, don't be naïve. He just did it for the money you gave him. That's all the kid cares about. That's why he dated Anna Catherine in the first place and got her pregnant. He knew who she was and wanted the money."

"I really don't think…."

"I told you to wait for me to get back. Now, look at what you have done!"

"And let the baby die?"

"It's not like he did anything to help her."

"I really…we need to get her to a hospital," Doctor Holden said. "There isn't much I can do to help."

"Shut up," Amelia said.

"She needs surgery," he continued.

Amelia grabbed the gun from her husband's hand. She walked to the doctor and placed it in his back. "Make her well. Do you hear me?"

"Y-yes."

"Good."

A loud crash echoed in the house and up the hallway. Amelia and Ron exchanged a look of panic. Voices bellowed below.

"FBI, we're coming in."

"What do we do?" Ron asked.

Amelia looked confused. Dr. Holden was panting and agitated, standing by the changing table, where he was trying to help the baby's heart pump, massaging her chest, while crying helplessly.

"I can't," he moaned. "I don't know…I can't…."

"What can't you?" Amelia asked.

"She's…she's slipping…."

"FIX HER!" she yelled and placed the gun to the doctor's head.

He turned to face her, his hands shaking.

"I can't. Don't you get it?"

She looked down at the tiny baby. Her chest wasn't moving.

Dr. Holden looked up at her, tears springing from his eyes.

"I'm so…sorr…."

"Don't say it," she said and walked closer, then pushed him aside. "She's not dead. I know she isn't. I can get her back. I can save her. There's still hope. There always is. It's not over. It's NOT over, I tell you!"

Chapter 72

I HEARD voices coming from up the stairs, then hurried to the staircase. I called Walsh from my phone, telling her to get there asap while rushing up, taking two steps at a time. I had completely forgotten I had been hurt, and all pain disappeared when the wave of adrenalin ran through my body.

The voices started yelling. They sounded panicked.

I hurried to the end of the stairs, then followed the sound of the voices. They were coming from the master bedroom, and they were getting louder.

"DO SOMETHING!"

I felt the badge in my hand. The leather was melted on the edges from being in my pocket during the explosion. Other than that, it had survived surprisingly well—same as my gun and even my phone. It was miraculous, but then again, they said the same thing about me. I had lucked out.

I pulled the gun out of the holster then took a deep breath. I peeked through the doorway. I saw three people inside the bedroom: Senator Hartnett, her husband Ron Hartnett, and a man

I didn't recognize. He was bent over the changing table and a small bundle.

Was he crying?

Oh, dear.

"Don't just stand there," Senator Hartnett yelled at him, going all up in his face. "Do something! You're a doctor. Save her!"

The doctor shook his head in desperation and took a step back. "I...There's nothing more I can do."

Senator Hartnett was almost screaming when she spoke next, "Yes, there is! Yes, there is! There has to be!"

That's when I saw the gun in her hand and clutched mine, then lifted it. She turned and saw me. I signaled for Alex to stay covered behind me.

"FBI," I said. "Put down the weapon."

Senator Hartnett gave me a stare, narrowing her eyes. The gun was shaking in her hand.

"I know you!"

"And I know everything you've done," I said. "How you stole Clarissa Smalls from the hospital in Florida and brought her back here, making sure she was found at the mall, then pretended like she was actually yours. How you kept her as your daughter for fourteen years because you lost your own." I paused and looked at Ron. "My guess is you took the second child, Desiree, right? Dressed as a nurse, you just walked right in there and took the child, stating she needed tests done. You just didn't realize that this one has a bad heart and needs surgery."

"I kept telling them," the doctor said.

"Shut up!" Amelia Hartnett said. "All of you!"

"We need to get the baby to the hospital," I said, defying her. "I fear that it is already too late."

Senator Hartnett stared at me, then lifted the gun slightly, and before I could react, she fired it at me.

Chapter 73

IT WAS like a scene out of a movie. In fact, if I had seen it in one, I would have laughed and said that it was too unrealistic. Yet, it happened. I didn't see him, but I spotted a shadow in the corner of my eye as Alex jumped out from behind the door, then threw himself on top of me, pushing me to the floor.

The bullet hissed past me, almost grazing me before hitting the wall behind me in the hallway, shattering a picture frame hanging there. The picture of the happy Hartnett family on a beach somewhere fell to the ground with a thud.

I stared at Alex on top of me, his terrified eyes looking down at me.

"Are you okay?" he asked.

I nodded, my entire body shaking. Amelia Hartnett walked closer, pointing the gun at us, then cocked it. I prepared for another shot being fired and looked for my gun, but it had fallen and slid to the doorway when I was pushed.

"Please," Alex said.

Senator Hartnett pointed the gun at us, first at him, then at me.

"I don't know who to finish off first," she said. She moved it back to Alex. "You're on top, so I'll start with you."

I closed my eyes, bracing myself, my heart hammering in my chest, when a noise coming from the hallway made Amelia Hartnett look up. Someone was there, but I couldn't see who it was because Alex was still on top of me. But I recognized her by her voice.

"Mom? What are you doing?"

I had to see if I was right and managed to lift my head just enough to see her. Clarissa stood in the doorway, staring at Amelia.

"C-Cate?" Amelia said, then clutched her chest. She looked briefly at her husband. "You're…you're alive?"

"Spare me," the girl said. "You know very well that I survived. I thought you would come for me. I waited in that godforsaken hospital for days, but you never came. Why?"

"We couldn't," Ron said. "We couldn't get to you. There were police everywhere."

Clarissa glared at the baby on the changing table. "Whose child is that? Is she supposed to replace me? What does this mean? It is true, then? They were right when they told me I had been taken? I thought they were lying. But I guess they weren't? I protected you two. I thought you loved me. I thought that falling off the airboat in the swamps was an accident, but it wasn't, was it? You wanted to get rid of me. You wanted me to die out there."

Ron shook his head. "N-no, sweetie, no, that's not true. We were on vacation and rented an airboat. You fell in while we were out there. We searched for you for a very long time."

"Really?" she asked. "That's odd. Because nowhere in the media have I read about the missing child of a senator. There is nothing anywhere about the famous Senator Hartnett's teenage daughter that went missing in the swamps of Florida. That's kind of strange, don't you think?"

"We didn't want the press to know," Ron said. "You must understand that. They would eat us alive. We simply told the people closest to us that you had run away with a boy if they asked where you were. We couldn't have that scandal...."

She shook her head, tears springing to her eyes.

"I don't believe you. You wanna know what I think? I think you couldn't deal with the scandal of me being pregnant at fourteen. It would ruin your career, and maybe it would even somehow be revealed who I really was, so you decided to replace me."

Amelia Hartnett looked at Ron, then at Clarissa.

"The doctor took a blood sample. It was AB. Ron and I are both blood type O. You couldn't be our child, or it is very unlikely, at least. We knew you'd find out at some point, and then what? It would have ruined everything. Plus, the baby thing...."

"I can't believe you," she said, shaking her head. "I thought...I thought we were a family?"

"We were," Ron said, clasping his chest. "We did love you. I love you. You will always be my daughter. It was Amelia who...who...."

He stopped when receiving a look from his wife.

"It doesn't matter anymore," Amelia said. She glared at the baby, then at her husband. "The child is dead. There's nothing more we can do for her."

Her manic eyes fell on me. The gun was still in her hand, and she pointed it at her daughter.

"No, you don't!" Ron yelled, coming up from behind her. "I let you try to kill her once before, and it has been a nightmare for me."

Amelia Hartnett began to cry, sobbing helplessly. The gun in her hand was shaking, and she bit her lip hard.

"I can't do it," she said, shaking her head.

Then she turned on her heel and fired at her husband instead. The bullet hit him in the chest, and he fell to the floor. Clarissa screamed.

"No! Dad, no!"

Amelia then turned the gun on herself and pulled the trigger. The gun clicked, but nothing happened.

She had run out of bullets.

Seeing this, I jumped to my feet, pushed Alex to the side, and leaped for her. She turned around and went for the window. She pulled it open, and before I could get to her, she jumped.

Chapter 74

I WATCHED HER DISAPPEAR. I reached the window, then stuck my head out just in time to see her roll down the side of the roof, then slide over the edge and land in the snow in the yard below.

She laid still for a few seconds, and I worried she had been hurt, but then she sat up and brushed snow off her arms and head before getting to her feet again and starting to run.

"I'll be...she's getting away!"

For a second, I considered jumping out after her, but Alex came up behind me and grabbed my collar, then pulled me back in.

"It's not worth it. You getting hurt is not worth it, Eva Rae."

"But...she's running. She's escaping...?"

I growled, annoyed as I watched Amelia stride through the snow in the backyard, getting closer to the exit at the end.

"See, she can get out down there and into the road behind it, and then she'll be gone," I said. "We'll never catch her. I'm not just gonna let her get...."

I stopped when seeing something out of the corner of my eye—a movement, a shadow springing in from the side, moving very fast toward Amelia Hartnett. She had obviously not seen this movement coming toward her and had slowed down, probably to catch her breath. Running in the snow was hard. Meanwhile, the shadow storming toward her didn't seem to be slowed down by it at all. Like a jack out of a box, it leaped at her, and they tumbled into the snow below, Amelia letting out a loud yelp. There was fighting in the yard, punches flew, and Alex and I stared at the scene with bated breath.

"What in…who is that?" I asked.

As I did, the person slammed a fist into Amelia's face, and suddenly she laid completely still—knocked out.

On top of her, the woman breathed heavily, then lifted her head and looked up toward me and smiled.

I couldn't believe it.

"Linda Smalls?"

I heard sirens and guessed it was Walsh that had arrived. I grabbed my phone, called her, and then told her to go into the backyard. I watched them storm toward Linda Smalls and Amelia Hartnett a second later, then arrest them both. I pulled my head back inside. Alex was sitting, bent over Ron, feeling for a pulse. He shook his head, and I turned to face the doctor, who was standing pale and paralyzed with the baby in his hands.

"She's…she's not breathing anymore, and I can't…there's no pulse. There is nothing more we can do."

"I called for an ambulance; it should be on its way," Alex said.

"It's too late," the doctor said. "It's over."

I rushed to the doctor then took the baby in my hands. She felt no heavier than a bag of nuts. My heart could barely bear it. I looked at Alex, tears springing to my eyes.

"I can't…I…."

He placed a hand on my shoulder for comfort. I was staring at Desiree in my hands, shaking my head, refusing to believe I was too late. It was too much to bear. I was so profoundly heartbroken.

I placed a hand on her chest then caressed her while the tears rolled down my cheeks.

And then I felt it.

It was faint, but it was there.

I lifted my gaze and met Alex's eyes.

"I felt something. I think it was a pulse."

Alex was barely breathing.

"Walsh is downstairs," I said. "She can take us to the hospital. I refuse to give up on her now. Let's go!"

Chapter 75

I SAT in the waiting room all night, bawling my eyes out. Alex was by my side, bringing me coffee that I barely touched while we waited for news of baby Desiree. Walsh had driven like a maniac through town with full blasting sirens, and it hadn't taken many minutes to get her to the hospital. Here, they had agreed that there was a faint pulse and rushed her into surgery.

Now, we were waiting for them to give us news. They had told us upfront that chances were small that she would make it—almost non-existent were their words. Still, I had that small hope inside me that refused to let go. I had finally found baby Desiree; it couldn't all have been for nothing.

They had to save her. They simply had to.

I was biting my nails.

"You never asked me how I found out where you were or how I figured out about Steve Melton, Sr. being a suspect," Alex said.

I sipped my coffee and looked up at him. "Are you trying to make small talk so I will think about something else?"

He smiled, exhausted but handsome as always. "So what if I am?"

"That's sweet of you," I said, "but I already know how you knew."

"Really?" he gave me a suspicious look. He shook his head. "No, you don't. You're bluffing me."

"Maybe I am," I said. "But maybe I'm not."

He grimaced.

"Okay, so, tell me what you know."

"Matt," I said. "My ex."

Alex almost dropped his cup. His eyes grew wide.

"How did you know?"

"It's simple, really. A friend of mine saw you drinking coffee together at Juice N' Java in Cocoa Beach. He sent me a picture of the two of you together a few days ago. It wasn't hard to figure out that you have been pumping him for information. He is, after all, the only one who knows where I am all the time. He's a wonderful guy but way too trusting. Meanwhile, you're a snake who knows how to get people to talk without realizing they are spilling secrets. Believe me. I figured you out long ago."

"I'll be…. Here, I got this entire thing prepared about how clever I was and figured things out on my own, and then you….."

"Oh, you're not fooling me. You got no secrets from me, my friend," I said. "And especially not in Cocoa Beach. It's a small town. You burp, and I'll know about it within the hour, including knowing what you had to eat. It's what I love and hate about the town."

He nodded and sipped his cup. "I'm impressed you figured it out, and that doesn't happen very often, I must admit. It's kind of hot."

I sent him a look, lifting my eyebrows.

"I'm not even gonna dignify that with an answer."

I looked down, trying to hide that his remark had made me blush.

The door swung open, and I forgot everything about blushing

and smart remarks. The doctor stepped out, an exhausted look on his face.

Alex and I both got up. I held my breath as the doctor came closer. I felt Alex's hand in mine, squeezing it tight.

The doctor exhaled deeply, then smiled.

"She's stable. We fixed the heart defect. Now, the next twenty-four hours will show if she'll make it—if she's strong enough."

I looked at the doctor, then up at Alex. I wasn't certain I had heard it right and needed his confirmation. The relief in his eyes told me I wasn't imagining things.

"She's…alive?"

"She's still alive, yes. And there is a real chance that she might survive if she makes it through the night. I understand that the mother is on her way here?"

"Yes, we called her, and she's getting on the first plane here with her mom."

"I hope we will be able to reunite mother and daughter in the morning, then. I will keep you updated," he said, then looked at his watch and left with a nod.

I turned to face Alex. He grabbed both my hands in his. I couldn't stop crying; I couldn't help myself. Even though I knew it was silly, it was just such an emotional moment. Alex felt it, too, and looked into my eyes. He then grabbed my face between his hands and wiped away a tear with his thumb while looking deeply into my eyes.

We stared into each other's eyes for a long time before I grabbed his neck and pulled him into a kiss.

Chapter 76

"KNOCK. KNOCK."

I peeked my head into the room. Linda Smalls was lying in her hospital bed and lifted her head when she saw me.

I smiled. She smiled nervously back, and I walked inside.

"What are you doing here?" she asked.

"I've been here all night, waiting for news about baby Desiree. They did her surgery, and she made it through the night, which is a miracle, they keep saying. Her mom, Sierra, just got here, and I left Desiree in her care."

"She got her baby back?" Linda asked. "That makes me very happy. Thanks for letting me know. At least she won't have to go through what I did. It wasn't all in vain then."

"Yeah, I wanted to thank you for that—stopping Amelia Hartnett the way you did and taking a beating. How are you feeling?"

She shrugged and lifted her cuffed hands. The handcuffs rattled against the bed. "They say I have a concussion, so for now, I'm just here. There's no saying where I will be tomorrow—probably in a jail somewhere. It's okay. I deserve it for what I did. Don't do the crime if you can't do the time, right?"

"I hear Steve Melton, Sr. is doing better, though," I said. "He will be able to walk again after rehabilitation."

She scoffed. "Yeah…I'm…"

She paused and looked down.

"And Trent? What will happen to him?" I asked.

"My sister will take him in. I just feel awful that I will miss years of him growing up, and I will never get to know my daughter. I really messed everything up."

"Speaking of," I said. "There's someone here to see you."

I walked to the door and opened it, then signaled for her to come inside. Linda sat up straight in the bed. She gasped when she saw Clarissa walk in. Clarissa lifted her hand to greet her.

"H-hi."

"I didn't come up with this," I said. "She was the one who wanted to see you."

"W-why?" Linda asked.

Clarissa shrugged. "I…I don't know. I was curious, I guess. To meet the woman who took down my kidnapper. To meet my real mom."

Linda was holding back her tears now but not doing a very good job. "I…I am no…."

Clarissa walked closer. "Hero? No. I know about the other stuff you did. But you did it because of me…to revenge me, and that's, well…I guess I just wanted to look into your eyes."

Their eyes met, and Linda smiled widely. "I don't even know what to call you. What name do you go by these days? Catherine? That's what they called you, right?"

"Cate," she said. "That's what people usually call me."

"Oh. Okay. Cate."

"But I think I might change it to Clarissa," she said. "It's kind of growing on me."

Linda lit up with a smile, then grew serious again.

"I'm going to jail. You know that, right?"

She nodded. "You're still my mom, and I'm going to stay with Emma...."

Linda nodded. "My sister."

"I just met her, and we had a long talk. I don't know her, but I think we can figure it out. She will help with the pregnancy and the baby once it gets here and help me get back to school to get an education. I'm thinking of becoming a midwife because I wanna help babies come into the world. I think that's pretty cool. And I have a brother now, who I will get to know, so that's cool too. And Steve will come to Florida too, he said. He wants to be a part of the child's life. And then when you come back out again, you'll have an entire family waiting for you, even a grandson."

Linda clasped her mouth.

"It's a...it's a boy?"

Clarissa nodded then touched her stomach.

"It is."

"That's amazing," Linda said. "You're gonna make a wonderful mother."

Clarissa walked closer. She was hesitant at first, but then she reached out her hand and touched Linda's.

"I'll come to visit. Me, Trent, and the baby," Clarissa said.

"We've lost so much time," Linda said between pressing back sobs.

"We'll figure things out. Somehow," Clarissa said.

Linda broke into tears now, and Clarissa pulled her into a deep hug. At first, it seemed uncomfortable for her, but then she seemed to relax. I decided that was my cue to leave.

Give them some privacy to get to know one another before they were once again split apart.

Epilogue

Three days later

I WAS SITTING at the gate, my suitcase next to me, my phone in my hand. I had been texting with my children all morning, updating them on my flight that kept being delayed because of heavy snowfall. It had been crazy with all this snow, and I was looking forward to getting back to sunny, warm Florida.

But most of all, I was dying to be with my kids again. I was especially looking forward to holding Angel, my sweet baby, in my arms again.

"Is this seat taken?"

I looked up from my phone and saw Alex standing in front of me. I blushed. I hadn't seen him since I left the hospital. I had spent days finishing up all the paperwork and leaving the case in the hands of Walsh, who would take over from now on. My job was done. Amelia Hartnett had admitted to everything during the first interrogation, even the fact that she had paid off someone at the lab to forge her DNA test fourteen years ago.

"What are you doing here?"

"This is my gate."

"You're going to Orlando?"

He sat down in the chair next to me, placing his messenger bag on the ground. He nodded.

"Why?" I asked.

I had regretted kissing him for every minute since I did it. It just complicated everything, and I was actually looking forward to leaving the town where he lived. Now, he was coming back with me?

I stared at his lips and suddenly felt the desire to kiss them again, then looked away.

No, Eva Rae. It's too complicated.

"So…I heard that you found the guy who took Hartnett's baby fourteen years ago?" he asked.

I stared at him. "Is that why you're on this plane? To pump me for information?"

"It's not like it's a secret," he said.

He was right. It would be in the papers soon, and he might as well be the one to write it.

"We found the remains in the backyard."

"How did you know where to look for it?"

I looked down. "I really don't want to talk about it."

He nodded. "I see. It was the ex-boyfriend, right? So, you're angry with yourself because he was a suspect back then? Because your detectives actually went to talk to him but didn't find the baby? Because you almost had him but decided not to pursue that angle. Is that it?"

I exhaled and closed my eyes briefly. "I told them not to focus on him," I said. "I told them to focus on the dad. It was all my fault. And then it caused this huge ripple effect of events through almost fifteen years. It destroyed so many lives. Just because of what I did."

I paused to swallow the growing knot in my throat. "I've been thinking of nothing else since we found the remains in Tom Wilder's backyard, and they were taken in for DNA testing and showed up as a match for the real baby Anna, the Hartnett's missing daughter. I can't stop thinking about how this is all my fault. Linda lost her child; Ron Hartnett is dead; Rivers almost died."

"He didn't, though. He woke up. He will be okay, they say," Alex said.

"He'll never work as a cop again," I said. "That's not okay. I did that. I destroyed his life."

He grabbed my hand in his and forced me to look into his eyes.

"You can't think like that. We all make mistakes. You taught me that, remember? Or was that just talk?"

"Mine just caused so much suffering."

"Mine did too. You and I are the same."

That made me laugh out loud.

"We are so not the same."

The flight attendant told us we were boarding, and I rose to my feet, then walked onboard. We sat at different ends of the plane, so I didn't see Alex until we got back out in Orlando, and I was waiting for my Uber outside.

"You wanna share a ride?" he asked. "We're going the same way."

I looked at the huge suitcase in his hand that he had just picked up from the conveyer belt inside. My Uber drove up to the curb, and we both got inside while the driver put Alex's suitcase in the back. We took off toward Cocoa Beach.

"It sure looks like you intend to stay for a little more than just a few days," I said as we reached the bridges leading to the barrier islands.

He smirked. "Yeah, well...maybe I might hang around for a little while. I have a feeling there might be more stories to tell if I stay close to you. For some reason, the mysteries seem to follow you wherever you go."

I gave him a look as the driver swung onto A1A, and we passed the city limit sign telling us we were now entering Cocoa Beach.

"Is that your way of asking me out on a date?"

He laughed. "Well, technically, we already kissed, so...and I *have* seen you naked. I think that makes us at least third date material."

I turned away from him, looking out the window as my small town passed. "You're so full of it."

We didn't say anything else until the driver drove onto my street and stopped in front of my house. I was about to leave the car when he grabbed my arm.

"Is that a yes? To a date?"

I exited the car then paused.

"Let's call it a *maybe*."

His eyes lit up. "This Saturday?"

"Show up at seven o'clock, then we shall see."

LITTLE DID SHE KNOW

I slammed the door shut and couldn't stop smiling as I walked up to the house. My son Alex was the first one who saw me. He came running toward me, and I grabbed him in my arms, even though he was getting too heavy for me. He was still my little baby.

"You gotta see *Livvie*," he squealed.

That was his nickname for his oldest sister.

"Olivia? Why?"

I lifted my gaze and spotted my daughter on the stairs as she walked down.

"Wow," I said. "You look amazing. Is this the...?"

She stared at me, and I could see how nervous she was.

"Yes, this is my outfit for prom. It's tonight."

I stared at my daughter with her short hair and black suit and tie. I could tell she was worried about my reaction to the fact that she wasn't wearing a huge prom dress. And I had to admit; it took a few seconds for me to adjust to the idea that I wouldn't get to see her in one.

I swallowed, pressing back a tear. Then, I smiled widely, pulling her into a hug.

"I think you look amazing."

THE END

Afterword

Dear Reader,

Thank you for purchasing *LITTLE DID SHE KNOW* (Eva Rae Thomas #10). I hope you enjoyed it. The idea for this book came when I read about a Florida mom who got her daughter back after 18 years. The child was kidnapped at the hospital when only eight hours old. The mom waited for so many years to get her daughter back, but when she finally did, the daughter didn't want anything to do with her and kept saying that the woman she grew up with, the one who had kidnapped her, was her real mom. The mother's frustration was so deep and interesting that I knew I had to write about it.

You can read more here:

https://www.firstcoastnews.com/article/entertainment/television/programs/gmj/kamiyah-mobley-rebuilds-strained-relationship-with-her-biological-mother-shanara/77-7cd53d74-fbbd-4740-bf91-dcbb3731243b

As always, thank you for all your support. Please leave a review if you can.

Take care,

Afterword

Willow

About the Author

Willow Rose is a multi-million-copy best-selling Author and an Amazon ALL-star Author of more than 80 novels.

Several of her books have reached the top 10 of ALL books on Amazon in the US, UK, and Canada. She has sold more than three million books all over the world.

She writes Mystery, Thriller, Paranormal, Romance, Suspense, Horror, Supernatural thrillers, and Fantasy.

Willow's books are fast-paced, nail-biting, page-turners with twists you won't see coming. That's why her fans call her The Queen of Scream.

Willow lives on Florida's Space Coast with her husband and two daughters. When she is not writing or reading, you will find her surfing and watch the dolphins play in the waves of the Atlantic Ocean.

Join Willow Rose's VIP Newsletter to get exclusive updates about New Releases, Giveaways, and FREE ebooks.
Just scan this QR code with your phone and click on the link:

SCAN ME

Win a waterproof Kindle e-reader or a $125 Amazon giftcard! Just become a member of my Facebook group **WILLOW ROSE - MYSTERY SERIES.**
Every time we pass 1000 new members, we'll randomly select a winner from all the entries.

To enter, just tap/click here:
https://www.facebook.com/groups/1921072668197253

Tired of too many emails? Text the word: "willowrose" to 31996 to sign up to Willow's VIP text List to get a text alert with news about New Releases, Giveaways, Bargains and Free books from Willow.

Follow Willow Rose on BookBub here: https://www.bookbub.com/authors/willow-rose

[Follow Willow on BookBub]

Connect with Willow online:
https://www.facebook.com/willowredrose
https://twitter.com/madamwillowrose
http://www.goodreads.com/author/show/4804769.Willow_Rose
https://www.willow-rose.net
Mail to: contact@willow-rose.net

Printed in Great Britain
by Amazon